HUCKLEBERRY JUJU
and Other Narrative Spells

by

David Bowles

HUCKLEBERRY JUJU
and Other Narrative Spells

by
David Bowles

FLOWERSONG
PRESS

MCALLEN, TX

ISBN 13: 978-1-963245-56-1

FLOWERSONG
PRESS

Published by FlowerSong Press
in the United States of America.
www.flowersongpress.com

TABLE OF CONTENTS

ACKNOWLEDGEMENTS

- "Huckleberry Juju" was previously published in *New Myths* #38, April 2017.
- "Oscar and the Giant" was previously published in *Juventud! Growing up on the Border*, edited by René Saldaña, Jr. and Erika Garza-Johnson; VAO Publishing, 2013.
- "The Body by the Canal" was previously published in *Living Beyond Borders: Growing up Mexican in America*, edited by Margarita Longoria; Viking Books for Young Readers, 2021.
- "The Boo Hag" was first published in the August 2016 edition of *Stupefying Stories*.
- "El Sombrerón" was previously published in *Both Sides: Stories from the Border*, edited by Gabino Iglesias; Agora Books, 2020.
- "When the Sky Fell" was previously published in *A Larger Reality 2.0: A Timeline in Which We Don't Go Extinct*, edited by Libia Brenda; ODO Ediciones, 2019.
- "The Challenge" was previously published in the 2016 edition of *Chachalaca Review*.
- "Ephemera" was previously published in the October 2016 edition of *Swords and Sorcery Magazine*.
- "Quintessence" was previously published in Volue 12, Issue 1 of *Electric Spec*, 2017.

- "Shrine" was previously published in *Road Kill: Texas Horror by Texas Writers*, edited by ER Bills and Bret McCormick; Eakin Press, 2016.
- "The Teen and the Triton" was previously published in *Mummies and Mermaids: A Strange Texas Tales That Never Die Anthology*; Overlooked Books, 2014.
- "To Brave the Mountains" was previously published in edition #15 of *SQ Mag*, 2017.
- "Shattered Intaglio" was previously published in *Castle of Horror Anthology Volume 9: YA*, edited by Jason Henderson and In-Churl Yo; Castle Bridge Media, 2022.

DEDICATION

For all the rootworkers and curanderas who kept the dark at bay.

HUCKLEBERRY JUJU

I T WAS LATE AUGUST WHEN THE WHITE FOLKS MOVED IN.

To be sure, the kids were half Cuban or Mexican or something Latin, but the mama was white for sure. They had been living on the base on Parris Island; then the daddy shipped out on an aircraft carrier headed to New York and the mama decided she needed to be away from all that military hustle and bustle, so lo and behold she found a mobile home at the heart of Frogmore on St. Helena.

It was a clean, sturdy trailer, one of about a dozen sitting on a couple of acres owned by my parents, Mr. and Mrs. Franklin Bailey, whose home spread spacious under the oaks and Spanish moss not a hundred yards from their tenants. Now, couldn't two people on earth be more different than my mama and daddy. Franklin Bailey had been a studious, quiet boy, and had grown into an accountant, of all things, with an aptitude for numbers that helped him manage his own rental properties as well. Amelia Shaw had once been the loveliest Gullah girl in all the Lowcountry, daughter of the slickest conjure man on St. Helena—John Arthur Shaw, more commonly known as Dr. Crow.

Well, though my daddy was an African Baptist who didn't much truck with hoodoo, he fell in love, hard, and he was willing to ignore mama's dabbling in green magic from time to time so long as she didn't bring her "witch-doctor daddy" by the house for supper.

Then I was born, a caul covering my face. The midwife slit holes for me to breathe through, gently unlooped the membrane from my head. It was fused to my skin a bit and had to be sliced carefully away—I still have small scars just behind each ear.

Everyone whispered about me. Such births are rare. Intense juju, you see. Granddaddy in particular was very intrigued, wanted me as his apprentice when I came of age.

All this is so you'll understand what happened, of course. It's context.

Garza. That was their last name. Three boys, all adrift without their daddy. Oscar must have been about eight, Samuel six. The little one, Fernando, he was just a toddler, always clinging to his mama's bell-bottom jeans.

I'd been watching them wandering dumbly through their little yard, kicking at dirt clods all sullen and dull. Not sure why I felt so bad for them. I was twelve, and you know how it usually goes—the younger ones come around like puppies, trying to get the attention of the big dogs. But my heart's not built that way. I wanted to help them.

I kind of towered over them, so it was nice to see they didn't shy away. "Hey, there. I'm Kenneth. What are y'all doing?"

The oldest peered at me from beneath his mop of copper hair with clever brown eyes. "I'm Oscar. This is my brother Sammy. We're just exploring and playing make-believe."

"Yeah? What are y'all pretending?"

"That this is a desert isle. Some pirate shipwrecked off the South Carolina shore centuries ago. Buried treasure here, Spanish gold and stuff."

"Cool," I told him. "Reminds me of something me and my daddy do. Want to come over to my house and check it out?"

Little Sammy sneezed. Kid had bad allergies, I found out later. His green eyes were always bloodshot like a drunk. "Need to tell mom, Oscar."

"Let me ask her," I said. I knocked on the door, and Mrs. Garza leaned out. She was small and pretty clearly Boston Irish, from her red hair to her Yankee accent.

"Hey, there. Can I help you?"

"I'm Kenneth Bailey, ma'am. My daddy's, you know…"

She smiled. "My landlord? Yup. Good man. Little serious."

"That's for sure," I laughed. She put you at ease, did Mrs. Garza. Didn't seem to faze her at all that I was a black kid, not the way I've seen my presence stiffen the back of many a white woman before and since. Maybe it's because her husband was Latin. "I was wondering if you'd allow Oscar and Sammy to come over to my house for a bit, to play and watch some TV."

"Oh, gosh, could they? That would be wonderful, Kenneth. They've been getting on my last nerve with their antics, and me with a two-year-old underfoot."

"I understand, ma'am. My own mama's got a little one, a baby girl. A real handful. I'll entertain these goobers for a couple of hours, don't you worry."

We walked through several empty lots back to my house. I showed them in, introduced them to my mama, who was still as lovely as ever, even at thirty-two and just a few months out from my sister's birth. She gave us each a glass of sun-brewed tea, and I took the boys into the living room, where my daddy had set up on shelves the fruit of our long, patient labor.

"Ships in bottles!" Oscar exclaimed with delight, a big smile lighting up his face.

Sammy wanted to look closely at each one, asking what sort they were, how we had managed to get them inside.

"Magic," I said, laughing, and he cocked his head at me all peculiar. "Just kidding. Lots of patience and special tools. Maybe y'all can come over next time we work on one."

They noticed our console TV with excitement, and we sat down to watch a re-run episode of that Planet of the Apes mini-series. I showed them my Red Ryder BB Gun and my daddy's boat before walking them back home. I tried to teach them some cool handshakes, but they fumbled around and made me smile at their clumsiness.

"Y'all come over tomorrow," I told them before I left. "It'll be Saturday, and we can watch Godzilla and Tarzan and all them great cartoons."

That's how it started. Like a ritual. The next two weeks, the very last of our summer vacation, we hung out every day. Oscar and Sammy would come over, maybe watch a little TV, shoot at cans in the yard, play with my Matchbox cars.

What they really liked was exploring.

My daddy's property stretched pretty far beyond the trailer park, and it was neighbored on two sides by even bigger tracts of empty, marshy land. We'd head out there, me with my Red Ryder across my arm, poking around the rusty carcasses of abandoned cars and looking for snakes. What surprised me was how much Oscar knew about plants and how interested he was in learning more.

"Our grandma's a curandera," Sammy said one day out of the blue when I was explaining about the curative prop-erties of a particular species of milkweed.

"Cállate, menso."

I didn't understand Spanish, but Oscar's look said everything.

"It's alright, Oscar. Y'all can trust me. What's he mean?"

Oscar's face flushed a bit. "It's supposed to be a family secret. She's a healer. Uses plants and magic. A shaman, they call them in books I've read."

I nodded.

"Right on. Very strange coincidence. My granddaddy, he's a root doctor, too. That's what we call them in these parts. Hoodoo men. Conjurers."

"Wow." Sammy's eyes were big as plates. Oscar visibly relaxed.

"Thought it was just a Mexican thing," he said. "Mom doesn't like to hear about it."

I laughed. "Yeah, my daddy don't like it much, either. Imagine how pissed he would be if he knew I was studying it."

"Get out," Oscar said, all incredulous.

In answer, I reached into my shirt and pulled out my conjure bag, a bit of red and white flannel in which some mugwort, Comfrey root and a piece of my caul had been sewn up. "Dig my mojo, boys. Some real potent juju in this thing."

"What's juju?" Sammy stretched his hand out, and I let him touch the conjure bag for a second before tucking it away again.

"It's like the magic all bundled up inside everything. Some things have more of it, but, yeah, man, juju is everywhere if you know how to look." I pointed at a nearby tree. "There's holy fire in them magnolia flowers."

Sammy, always serious, seemed fit to burst with excitement. "And these?" he asked, pointing to some ripe purple fruit in amongst the sweetgrass.

"Oh, hell, boy, those are huckleberries. You bet your ass there's juju in huckleberries!"

They laughed then, laughter that haunts me to this very day.

"I bet if I would eat enough of them, I'd be a root doctor, too!" Sammy shouted.

With a chuckle I tousled his mousy hair. "Just might, little man. Just might."

As fate would have it, that Saturday I went with my mama to visit my granddaddy, who pulled me off into his conjure shack to teach me the ends and outs of uncross-ing—removing a jinx from someone. Midway through the lesson he snatched my mojo out of my shirt with a bony hand and hissed in that Gullah-tinged dialect of his.

"Who you let touch you trick bag, huh? I smell he grubby hand right there! Not long enough for steal you power, but mayhap enough for turn you trick aside." He straightened, crossed his arms over his chest, tapping the lapels of his black suit with his long, yellow nails. "See them good. Was me fingers what sewed up that magic for protect you, you know this, yaas? Must not let no other body close to it."

I tried to explain. "It's just a little white boy. Got no daddy around. I've been showing him and his brother about plants and such."

"White boy?" Grandaddy tsked, adjusted the brim of his hat. "That's worse. Ain't no buckruh what can under-stand we traditions for true. Bad idea, that."

"Well, they're part Mexican or something. Their grandma, she's a conjure woman like you. They already got a little lore from their daddy."

"Rest you tongue. You unravel you mouth too much, boy. Must heed me words. No more sharing lore what ain't earned."

There was rage in his yellowed eyes. Everyone feared him, back in those days. I was no exception. "Yessir."

"Serious now, boy. You me grandson, but I'll cross you so hard ain't no way you could be unjinxed, hear?"

And that was it for my lesson. He told me to get out of his sight, and mama soon drove us home. Daddy was in a shitty mood like he always was when we came back from those "Geechee boondocks," and he gave me a long list of chores, including washing the cars and his boat, though we hadn't gone fishing in that thing for months.

So it was that I was hosing down the hull in tank top, cut-offs and ratty old sneakers when Oscar Garza came running up and changed my life forever.

"Kenneth!" he shouted. His eyes were wild with desperation and fear. "It's Sammy! Come quick!"

I dropped the hose and ran after him without a moment's hesitation. His frantic strides guided me beyond my daddy's land to a weed-infested husk of a Chevy Valiant. Sammy was lying atop some clumps of switchgrass, still as a corpse.

"You said you'd be gone," Oscar panted. "So I was just reading. In my room. Mom told me Sammy was gone. Went to look for him. Found him like this."

I dropped to my knees. Sammy's face was smeared with purple juice. I jerked my head up, flitted my eyes over everything.

That's when I saw the blood red vines of Virginia creepers, all over the trunk of the Valiant, heavy with purple fruit.

"Oh, shit!" I exclaimed. Seizing my conjure bag in my left hand, I closed my eyes and laid my right on Sammy's unmoving chest. I felt the eerie cold of a spirit fixing to leave its body. Panic rose to paralyze me, but I shoved it aside.

I was born with a damn holy caul upon my face. I'm hoodoo through-and-through. I can do this. I can bring him back.

"Oscar!" I leapt to my feet, turning to the car. "Bring me every loose piece of iron you see. Quick! We don't have much time!"

Between the two of us, we found five bits of metal I could use. I set them in the form of a quincunx around Sammy's corpse, trapping his essence like one might a haint.

"Okay, okay," I said, a little calmer. "We got us a few minutes. Not much more. Listen close, Oscar. You know that tree on the far side of my house, the one with a blue bottle hanging from a branch? Run and bring me that. Don't let my parents see you, now. Hurry!"

As he bolted, I squeezed some water from my damp tank top and cleaned the purple stain from the boy's lips, which were going blue right fine on their own now. I could feel the eternal part of him squirming there in my trap, confused and afraid, getting riled up fierce. Carefully as I could, I unstitched my conjure bag a smidge and pinched off a bit of my caul. Opening Sammy's mouth, I lifted his tongue and laid the shriveled-up scrap of membrane there.

I heard painful gasping behind me. Oscar fell down just beyond the quincunx, the bottle tumbling from his hand as his breath heaved mightily in his little chest. I snatched it up, glancing through the translucent cobalt blue at the afternoon sun. Mama had hung it up to stop evil spirits, but there was nothing trapped inside.

"Okay, Sammy," I said, raising my voice, which took on some of the rhythms of the root doctor I would one day become. "You done tried to get you some juju, son, but you ate the wrong berries. A little poison in each, and you wolfed down more than I can count. But I'm going to share my mojo with you, Sammy, and you're going to be just fine. Just come get yourself in this here bottle, now, and do it quick."

I closed my eyes, felt for that spirit, and drew it slow but sure with my right hand toward the broad opening of the bottle. A little reluctant, but recognizing me at some level, his essence slipped inside.

Dropping immediately beside Sammy's head, I tilted the bottle to his mouth, urging him back inside the flesh with every ounce of my will.

"God," I rasped, "and all His angels and all the mighty beings of the higher realms, help me restore this here little boy, who is blameless and pure in the eyes of heaven."

There was a moment when I was certain I'd failed, that I'd been judged at fault for this tragedy. Then the boy inhaled sharply and opened his eyes, more bloodshot than ever.

"Sick." It was just a whimper, rough and animal. I helped him sit up, and he vomited up what seemed a gallon of violet bile.

"Get him home," I told Oscar. "He should be okay. Tell your mama he had sunstroke or some-such. We'd both be in hot water if they found out what we've done."

He nodded his understanding, and they hobbled away. I high-tailed it over to my house, hung the bottle back up quick, finished my chores.

I guess I felt really good about myself, saving that boy.

The truth of the matter took some time to come clear.

School started, and the three of us rode on the same bus, though Oscar, Sammy and other grade-school kids got dropped off at the elementary before the bus swung by the junior and high schools to leave the rest of us. As they were the only white kids on the route, I let everybody know they were my friends. They were left alone, even by bullies. My granddaddy's reputation was good for that sort of thing.

Sammy, always a quiet boy, was now virtually mute. I reckoned he'd need some time to recover, but two weeks later, he was still shambling around like an old man.

Hoping to get him excited about something, I had the boys over on the Monday afternoon of the third week of school. A new Japanese cartoon called Battle of the Planets was premiering, and the commercials I'd seen for it looked righteous. But poor Sammy sat through the adventures of the G-Force without so much as a twitch or a smile.

"Something's really wrong with him, huh?" Oscar whispered to me during a commercial.

"Nah, man," I lied. "Death just takes a long time to get over. Quit your worrying."

But when Oscar wasn't looking, I yanked a strand of hair from his little brother's head. That night, locked in my room, I pried up a floorboard and pulled out my bowl of possum bones—specially marked and painted—and the casting cloth my granddaddy gave me when I began my apprenticeship.

My stomach clenched tight, I laid Sammy's hair at the center of the cloth and began my investigation. As I asked my silent questions, throwing the bones and again and again, I had my worst fears confirmed.

Nausea rising in my throat, I could almost hear my granddaddy snarl at me, his voice crackling in my head. "He ain't got no soul, Kenneth. You done return he spirit to that body yonder, but he soul gone and left this here world forever."

One of the first lessons. Body, spirit, soul. No man is complete unless he has all three. An animated body without a soul, without the personality that makes us who we are, well, there are lots of names for such a creature, but they all boil down to the same thing.

Undead.

I already knew the only solution. But I loved those boys, you understand, like they were my own kin. I couldn't do it. Couldn't tell anyone, either. Like my granddaddy used to say whenever it was time to keep some rootwork secret, "Every sick ain't for tell the doctor."

But Sammy got worse. Listlessness turned to aggression, mindless and mean. He attacked a boy at school, tried to bite a little girl. Horrified and confused, Mrs. Garza kept him at home.

"She has to lock him in her room," Oscar told me the very last time we ever spoke. "He tried to strangle Fernando, Kenneth. You need to tell me what the hell you did to him."

Ashamed and afraid of being found out, I turned on that child. It was cowardly, evil. But I tried to place the burden on his shoulders alone.

"This ain't got shit to do with me, Oscar," I snapped. "You're the one who let him go off alone. He's your little brother, man. You were supposed to look out for him, and you didn't. I saved him, best as I could. Now deal with the consequences."

His face. Oh, God, that little sun-burnt and freckled face, how it collapsed in on itself before he turned away, destroyed.

Not much else to tell. The father took leave from New York, came down to be with his family. There was nothing he could do, really. By late October, they had moved to the state capital. I later learned they checked Sammy into the Columbia Area Mental Health Center.

You know the rest, Detective. His parents left him there and eventually moved away. Their daddy was from Texas, so maybe that's where they ended up.

Here we are, thirty-five years later. The Center finally releases him, he comes back to St. Helena, and he takes those hostages in that diner across the street.

That's why you need to let me talk to him. He is incomplete, and there's nobody can stop him without collateral damage except me.

For the record? My name is Kenneth Bailey. I am a licensed practitioner of homeopathic medicine. Yes, of course that means I'm a rootworker.

That's correct. After he had interviewed me, Detective James Barnwell permitted me to cross over to the diner to see whether I could negotiate with Mr. Samuel Garza. Mr. Garza indicated to one of the hostages that she should let me in. As y'all know, three minutes later, the hostages exited the diner.

The body? There is no more body, gentlemen.

Yes, I'll explain. As soon as Mr. Garza—Sammy—saw me, he nodded almost violently, shaking his head up and down like an excited child. I walked straight up to him, took him in my arms. Big fellow, sure, but I gathered him up and squeezed him tight.

"Forgive me, Sammy," I whispered into his ear. Felt him loosen against me, ready.

I pulled back a bit, looked into those harrowed eyes, the green all swallowed up by a red the bloody shade of Virginia creepers. I remembered his trembling hand, reaching for my conjure bag. An ordinary boy, yearning for a little magic. I placed my hand across his forehead like a holy rolling preacher, then reached into him with my power and unbound his tortured spirit from that long-dead flesh.

Without a sound, he burst into ash. This dust y'all see covering my suit and hat? That's all that remains of Mr. Samuel Garza.

Go ahead, DNA test it. Sure.

Hold me for further questioning? Well, I suppose. Y'all can investigate all y'all want. My work can wait a few days while y'all spin your wheels.

Other aliases? Come on, son, what a question. Everybody on St. Helena knows who I am. Inherited the title from my granddaddy when he died.

They call me Dr. Crow.
I'm the Hoodoo Man.

OSCAR
AND THE GIANT

TOWARD THE END OF MY JUNIOR YEAR, THINGS GOT really bad. I mean, it was tough enough living in the projects, in one of the Section-8 apartments across the street from the Pharr Community Center, standing in for an absent dad with my little brother Fernando. Mom was working two jobs, my girlfriend had dumped me because I didn't have money to take her out, and the cheap guitar my cousin gave me had a warped neck. I thought life sucked about as bad as it could.

But then I went and insulted Bernard.

I was standing with some friends on the steps to the auditorium at PSJA High School one morning, the bus having dropped us off at an ungodly hour, like usual. A random assortment of cholos, preps and nerds made fun of my long hair and torn jeans as they passed. As usual. I was wearing these turquoise Converse high-tops that my mom had saved up to buy me, and that really got them going.

"Freak!" some of them jeered. "¡Pinche mariposón!" And those are some of the nicer epithets, believe me. I would normally just brush such insults off, but I don't know. Maybe because Diana had broken up with me, I just wasn't in the mood to be stepped on anymore.

So when Bernard Ayala came trouncing up the steps and muttered, "Out of the way, girlfriend," I snapped and yelled at the freshman.

"Hey, Bernard!"

He turned around, an eyebrow arched. "Yes, O Freaky One?"

"Nothing wrong with being gay," I told him despite the tightening in my stomach. I had been trying to ignore my own increasing attraction to boys for a couple of years. Still, I knew there was something particularly gross about confronting Bernard this way. "But do you have to be such a drama queen? It's getting really obnoxious."

Javi and Luis, my two best friends, looked at me like I had lost my mind.

Bernard's eyes narrowed. "Oh, Oscar Garza. You idiot."

And then he walked off.

"Oscar," Luis muttered, "you just insulted Simón Ayala's little brother, man."

I swallowed hard. Simón Ayala was the head of the Tri-City Bombers, the notorious street gang that managed petty crime in the Pharr-San Juan-Alamo area. He was in prison, but all the little wannabes at PSJA High School did his bidding, obeying whatever commands he sent through his lieutenants.

"I know." My voice trembled. "Pero me vale."

My bravery didn't last too long. The following day, there were no more insults. Instead, I was tripped, repeatedly, in the hallways. After that, I got my head slammed into a locker, twice. My Converse were stolen during PE, and I had to borrow Javi's extra shoes, a pair of Payless canvas slip-ons. Damián and Elías, a couple of 19-year-old sophomores, started following me everywhere. They had a host of new nicknames for me, including my favorite, güero cacahuatero. I would step out of class, and there they'd be, right behind me.

"¿Qué onda, güerito?" Damián would often say. "Got any clever remarks today, ese?"

"Yeah." Elías was a big brute who could only repeat his buddy's words. "What up, ese? We want to hear your clever remarks."

I knew better than to address them. They'd shove me from behind, or trip me, or slam me into a locker, but I kept my mouth shut. And I damn sure didn't go near a bathroom. That would have been suicidal. Grin and bear it, I told myself. You've been through worse.

Javi and Luis did what they could to help me. They convinced a lot of the wanksters to back off, that I wasn't worth the trouble. Luis was in JROTC, and he and his military-loving classmates intervened a couple of times, kept me from getting too hurt. But my friends couldn't always be around. We had different classes, and just when the attacks would seem to stop, out of nowhere Damián or Elías would appear to torture me some more.

If I can just make it through one last six weeks, I told myself. Summer will start, and I'll be free of them.

Finally, though, I saw Damián talking to Diana, his arm around her, right beneath the mesquite tree where I had asked her to be my chick. The flunky saw me looking and smiled like a happy predator.

I flipped him off.

When his face twisted in rage, I knew I had really screwed up. They would have probably gotten bored and forgotten about me, but now it was about Damián's honor and not just brown-nosing the boss-man. I almost skipped the rest of the day, but when I got close to the fence, Officer Limón yelled for me to get my butt back to class. So I did, and the hours dragged on in miserable anticipation.

After school I didn't see either of the goons. Looking back and forth to make sure, I made a beeline to the bus and slumped into my accustomed seat. Luis was at a JROTC fieldtrip and Javi was home sick, so I was alone today, able to stretch my legs out and relax for the ridiculously long bus ride home. As I got comfortable, I glanced at the back of the bus.

There they sat. Damián with a psychopathic grin on his face, Elías almost drooling in his Neanderthal idiocy. I quickly looked away, but I could feel their eyes on me during the whole roundabout journey, down 281 to Las Milpas, then a right on Dicker, stopping what seemed every ten feet to drop someone off, then another right to head north on Jackson. Finally the bus turned onto Kelly and hissed to a stop not far from the housing complex where I lived. We were the last ones on the bus. I got off and started walking as fast as I could without flat-out running. Even cowardly rockers have their pride.

"Where you going?" a voice crooned just over my shoulder, and one of the punks shoved on my books, sending them flying. I let them fall, beginning to run in earnest now. Forget pride, I thought. I don't want the crap beat out of me!

My feet pounded the asphalt of our parking lot. I made it to the stairs that led up to the second-floor apartment and dashed up to the landing, where I turned around and saw them looking up at me, laughing. All the crap that had happened to me over the past four years, all the rage I had pushed down deep in order to survive … all of it came bubbling to the surface, squeezing my chest and making my vision go hazy. The flunkies' jeers were like goads to a bull.

Without thinking, I struck out. I wanted to erase those smiles from their faces so badly.

I was outmatched physically, so I opened up my big, smart mouth and let them have it. "Ah, qué pobres mensos, los dos. You guys think you're so freaking bad, pushing me around at school, chasing me down, knocking my books out of my hands … it's pathetic. Son unos pinches perdedores. You're what … 19? And still sophomores? Why do you even bother? Yeah, maybe I live in the barrio and stuff, but do you really think I'm going to stay here? Have you seen my GPA? My ACT scores? I've got a life ahead of me. I'll go to college, get a good job, marry a beautiful girl. My life is going to be freaking awesome. ¿Pero ustedes? What are you going to do, huh? Keep collecting welfare? Knock up some desperate fourteen-year-old? Get a job digging ditches?" My hands were trembling, my mouth dry, my heart pounding. I felt dirty, but I went on. "You realize, right, that no one would miss you if you disappeared today? That your lives don't make a freaking difference to anything or anyone? Why don't you just kill yourselves now, get it over with? It's like you don't even exist."

Something horrible happened to Damián's face, as if every blood vessel in his forehead and temples was about to burst. Then he started coming up the stairs, crouched like a hungry predator. Luis circled around and came up the other stairwell, the two of them converging on the landing. I thought about heading to the apartment, but if Fernando wasn't there, I'd have to fish my key out of my pocket, and there just wasn't enough time. So I swung over the railing and dropped to the asphalt, backing away. They came back down, and Damián pulled a switchblade from his pocket.

"Pinche loco jodido," he spat. "Nobody talks to me like that."

I spun and ran like I had never done in my life, sprinting down Kelly and across the crazy late-afternoon traffic on Jackson. I risked a glance over my shoulder, but they were coming like hellhounds, closer and closer. I crossed a weedy field, heading toward the construction site near the expressway. Got to find something to defend myself with, I vaguely thought. My lungs were burning, and the muscles in my legs screamed at me to stop. Slipping under the perfunctory fence they'd put up, ignoring the danger signs, I jogged past back-hoes and cranes, scurried over piles of lumber, edged along mountains of dirt and cement block.

And then the ground went out from beneath me, and I fell.

I rolled over in the dust, trying to get my wind back. I had stepped too close to the excavations they'd made for the foundation of whatever building was going up at the site. As I got to my knees, looking around at the five-foot walls that surrounded the huge space, I noticed a strange outline in the dirt before me. It seemed as if I was crouching on the chest of some enormous, buried statue. Forgetting about my pursuers, I leaned forward and brushed red dust from what looked like its face: a broad forehead, a nose the size of my fist, a jutting chin.

When I drew my hand away, its eyes opened.

Startled, I scrabbled backward, moving away as quickly as I could in a crab-like scuttle. As my back hit the wall of dirt behind me, Elías and Damián leapt into the pit, chests heaving. They moved in. I was cornered.

"Ahora vas a ver." Damián gestured with his knife. "See if you still think you're all that with a couple holes in your chest, güey."

There was movement behind him: two massive hands, breaking free of the clay, pressing down on the packed earth, pushing a gigantic torso away from the ground.

"Dude," I said, pointing over Damián's shoulder, "You should probably look behind you."

"I look stupid to you?" Damián turned to Elías. "Agárrame a este pinche vato."

The figure emerging from the dirt was now sitting, the top of his head extending about a foot above that of Elías. Sand drained in rivulets down the giant's bare chest. His eyes narrowed as he focused on the scene in front of him.

Elías yanked me to my feet. I was too stunned to even attempt to pull away. Damián's blade flashed in the afternoon light.

"Think you got a life ahead of you, ese? Think again. A ver quién te extraña a ti, méndigo."

He swung the knife toward me, but his arm was suddenly jerked back. The giant had reached out and grabbed him, yanking him away from me. With a rumbling grunt, the enormous creature stood, rocks tumbling from what appeared to be leather leggings, stitched from a half-dozen different species of animal. Elías's hands slipped away from my shoulders. His jaw was wide open.

"What the…?" he managed to mutter. Damián struggled in the giant's grasp, looking like a rag doll or something. With his left hand, the strange being scooped up Elías, too, who began to make sobbing noises. After regarding them both for a few seconds, the giant set them on the edge of the excavation.

"Corred," he growled as he released them, and, man, did they run! I'm betting they didn't stop until they reached their homes in San Juan.

The giant then turned and looked down at me. He stood easily nine feet tall, pure brute muscle like carved granite, but his orange eyes were kind beneath a shock of white hair.

"Thank you," I croaked.

"You are welcome." His voice thrummed through the hard-packed earth like the best subwoofer in the Valley. "I could not permit them to attack. You are unarmed."

"You...you speak English."

"I am a tlacahueyac. A giant of the First Sun. The Feathered Lord gave my people the gift of languages when the world was young. I am able to converse with all thinking creatures."

The enormity of what was happening began to sink in. There is a freaking giant standing in front of me! My knees wobbled a bit.

"How ... how long have you been buried in the ground? How can you still be alive? I'm going crazy, right? Those losers knifed me, and I'm hallucinating as I bleed out."

The giant gave a soft, soothing laugh at my sudden panic. "No, human, you are not seeing visions. Nor have you been wounded. Let us begin again. My true name is beyond your ability to pronounce, but other humans once called me Olontetl."

He paused. I realized he was waiting for me to introduce myself. "Oh, I'm Oscar. Oscar Garza."

"Well met, Oscar. I am pleased you awakened me, if only to ward you from those fools. But I see my slumber has been long and humans are no longer accustomed to the sight of giants. If you will sit and rest for a time, I will briefly tell you my tale."

I slumped to the ground. He knelt and eased his bulk lower.

"In the First Age of the world, the Feathered Lord, creator and father, formed the white-haired giants. Sturdy as boulders, we went about the earth, taming its wildness and building wondrous works to glorify our maker. But the Lord of Chaos despised our fealty to his younger brother, and so he tempted many giants, transforming them into monstrous jaguars and setting them against their kin.

"It was a dark, dark time. My own father was turned, and he killed most of my family. I escaped with my brother, and we hid in the depths of the mountains for many years. When we emerged, we found our world destroyed; the strongest among us had wielded frightening, apocalyptic magic to defeat the jaguars, but they laid the earth to waste in the process.

"Only twelve of us remained. My brother and I. Ten others. The Feathered Lord drew us to his side and gave us a new commission: to defend his children against destruction. We would sleep for millennia, he told us, but when chaos rose again, we would be awakened.

"And so we passed the ages. I saw the Second Sun ended by the wrath of mighty hurricanes. The Third Age withered, ravaged by storms of angry fire. A flood effaced the world at the end of the Fourth, heralding the time of humans. We strove, we giants, against the devastation, but one by one we fell. Age after age we dwindled. For a time we would stave off the darkness. Order would be restored. We would sleep long centuries. But we always awakened to even greater chaos and despair. With every new era it has become more difficult to fight.

"At the beginning of this Fifth Age, only three of us remained. As humankind spread across the earth, we each went our separate ways, ever watchful. Many times have I been roused to avert chaos. Now you have called me from my dreamless resting, Oscar. You must lead me toward the wrongs that must be righted."

It was almost too much to take in. The story he told me was unbelievable, but there he knelt: an ancient giant, asking me to command him. I had been weak for so long that my mind boggled at the idea of such power.

The Tri-City Bombers, the drug traffickers, the child-abusers and wife-beaters … all the horrible things I've watched for years now … I can make them stop.

The sun was low in the sky. Fernando was probably worrying. He might even call mom, and she would take off from work at her second job to come looking for me. I needed to get back. But I couldn't take Olontetl with me. He was way too big, and I needed to prepare people first. Javi's uncle Pablo has a ranch in Hidalgo, I remembered. We could put Olontetl there for a while.

"Okay, I can do that." I stood and got closer to the giant. His breathing reminded me of gusty spring winds, blowing warmth through the mesquite trees, along the crabgrass. "But, Olontetl, you need to stay here another night, okay? I've to make arrangements, find … allies."

"Of course," he rumbled. "I will rest here until you return. Then we will engage the forces of the Lord of Chaos. Perhaps this time will be the last. Or perhaps I will fall, like my brother did at the end of the Third Age. But we fight, Oscar, because we must. Beauty and order, creation, and knowledge ... we cannot allow these to be swallowed up by destruction and entropy."

He placed a massive hand lightly on my head, and then he lay back down in the dirt, blending in so completely that I could only make him out by his bright orange eyes and snow-white hair.

"I'll be back in the morning," I promised, and I clambered out of the pit.

When I got home, Fernando was still at Speedy Espericueta's apartment, watching inappropriate movies on cable. He hadn't even noticed I wasn't in the apartment. It was Friday night, but I knew Javi and Luis would be home: they weren't as broke as me, but they didn't have girlfriends or cars, so it's not like they had a lot of choice.

"Dude," I told them both, "meet me outside tomorrow morning at like 8:30. I've got to show you something you are just not going to believe." They pestered me for more information, but I knew better than to tell them anything else. They wouldn't believe me without seeing for themselves. No one would.

It was hard going to sleep. I kept imagining Olontetl going up against gangbangers and drug dealers, pimps, and coyotes. Maybe even hunting down my dead-beat dad and taking care of him as well. Justice, I thought to myself over and over. Finally, justice.

Somehow, I fell asleep. The alarm went off at 8:15, and I got dressed and brushed my teeth. Mom was pouring herself a cup a coffee. She made a zombie-like movement to say good morning, and I waved distractedly as I rushed out the door.

Javi and Luis were a little late, like always. "So what's this top-secret shit you want to show us?" Javi asked, stifling a yawn.

"Just come on, dude. It's over at the construction site near the expressway."

I tried to get them to walk faster, but they ambled along casually, making stupid jokes at my expense. As we crossed the field, I heard the beeping sounds of heavy machinery, the barked orders of supervisors directing workers. *Oh, no*, I thought. *Why are they working on Saturday?*

Rushing to the excavation, I felt nausea rising in my gut. Two large cement trucks were pulling away, their rotating mixers visibly empty. As helmeted men yelled at me to stop, I ran to the edge of the pit and dropped to my knees in despair. It had just been filled with concrete, tons and tons of it, gleaming palely in the morning sun. Tubes jutted like gravestones from the vast, gray expanse.

"He's gone." A sob wracked my aching chest.

Javi and Luis caught up to me. "What, güey?" Javi demanded. "What are you freaking out about?"

"He's gone," I repeated. "And now I've got to face it all alone."

Luis knelt beside me. "Oscar, I don't know what's wrong, but you're not alone, man. Somos cuates, ¿que no? Me and Javi, we got your back, brother. We'll get those punks to back off, somehow. Now, come on, man. You're scaring me."

I stood and tried to casually wipe the tears from my cheeks. I looked at them both: the crazy military brat whose dad died in some foreign land, the scrawny migrant kid who lived half the year in Washington. I thought of my own self, a poor nobody with a brain but not much else. We weren't giants, the three of us. We probably didn't stand a chance against the darkness that assailed us.

But we would keep fighting.

THE BODY
BY THE CANAL

S EPTEMBER OF 1987 WASN'T MUCH DIFFERENT FROM
September of 1986. My dad was still gone, we were
still living on food stamps and welfare, I was still a
freak at my high school, trapped in this conservative
border town, unusual even for the circle of outcasts
that had formed around me. Every girl I dated ended
up dumping me. The teachers thought I was too smug
for my own good. I crossed out the days on my calendar, counting
down toward graduation. Escape.

Then the new neighbors moved in downstairs, and everything
changed.

It was a Saturday. Luis, Javi, and I were across the street at the
Pharr Civic Center, taking turns falling off a beat-up skateboard we'd
scammed off a rich white kid from McAllen.

"Is that a dude or a chick?" Luis asked.

I looked over at the thin, elegant figure struggling to pull a box
from the trunk of an old sedan. Longish hair teased wildly. Knee-
high boots with one-inch heels. Bangles, bracelets, and a bright pink
Swatch on the left wrist. A satiny black shirt with a frilly collar. Lips
bright with color. Eyelids shaded.

As out of place in this shitty neighborhood as a peacock among
chickens. I knew the feeling.

"I dunno," I said. But my stomach did a pirouette as the newcomer turned to look at us.

Boy or girl, the kid was beautiful.

And from my own experience, this town would do all it could to
destroy that beauty.

"Only one way to find out," Javi said, stamping on the back of the skateboard so it popped straight up. Snatching it from the air, he gestured with his chin. "Let's go say hello."

I was strangely conscious of my own appearance as we walked back across Kelly Avenue to the Section 8 apartments, where I lived with my mom and my little brother, Fernando. Torn Levi 501s. Turquoise canvas high-tops, off-brand. A random white T-shirt with purple blotches that had seemed gnarly when I bought it but now made me feel like a total poseur. Since it was Saturday, I hadn't bothered to curl the bangs of my bi-level hairdo, which reached my shoulders in back.

I figured I looked a mess. Still, I got out in front of Javi and Luis, anyway. They were a little ranchero, always putting their feet in their mouths when meeting cool people, even though they meant well.

"Hey," I said, waving as we approached. "Need any help?"

"Nah," the newbie said, and I could tell he was a guy though his voice was soft. The homophobes at our school were going to have a field day. "I've got it. Thanks."

"My name's Oscar, by the way," I added. "I live right above you, in 211. These are my friends Luis and Javi. They live . . . elsewhere."

I waved my hand vaguely, and he smiled. Glints of amber in his eyes caught the morning sun, sparkling like gold. My palms began to ache.

"Ariel," he said, pronouncing it in Spanish: ah-RYEL. "Ariel Ortega."

A glance told me that the box he was balancing on the bumper was full of records.

"Cool look," said Luis, who sported a crew cut because of JROTC. "Like a little punk, a little hair metal . . ."

"It's gothic," I said, and Ariel's honey eyes widened. "A bit more Siouxsie Sioux than Ian Curtis, but still."

Ariel tilted his head, and something fluttered in my chest. "Try Robert Smith. What was your name again?"

"Oscar," I said. "Oscar Garza."

There was a strange pause. Somewhere a whip-poor-will gave its plaintive cry. There was a skull ring on Ariel's right hand, I noticed. His fingers were slender and manicured.

"Welcome to Pharr, Texas, bro," Luis said. "We're sort of the outsiders at the high school, so, yeah. You'll eventually wind up with us three."

"Pardon me?" Ariel asked.

Javi gestured at the newcomer's clothes. "Let's just say you're not the typical student."

"But that's okay," I interjected, narrowing my eyes at my friends pointedly. "It's a backwoods rancho, but survivable. Just make sure the counselors put you in college prep classes with me."

"With us," Javi corrected. I heard him sigh, though I didn't look away from Ariel. Couldn't. There was a jingle as Javi fished his keys from his pocket. "Come on, Luis. I've got an afternoon shift at Starlite Burger. I'll drop you at your uncle's place on the way."

"Wait, what about . . ." Luis began, but Javi had already walked over to el Moco, his dad's green Impala. Luis glanced at Ariel and me. He took a knowing breath and nodded. "Órale, I'm coming. Nice meeting you, Ariel."

I ended up helping Ariel set up his stereo after his mom, Gloria, found us talking music outside and invited me to stay for lunch. She was pretty open about their situation: they'd been living in Austin, but Mr. Ortega was a drunken son of a bitch who wouldn't leave her precious boy alone. Rather than returning to California, where her family lived, she was trying to throw her abusive husband off the scent by coming to the Rio Grande Valley.

I had seen a couple of Cure videos on MTV, but I'd never listened to a full album, so Ariel lowered the needle on their latest: *Kiss Me, Kiss Me, Kiss Me.*

"When they toured with Siouxsie and the Banshees," Ariel explained, "Smith ended up taking over as guitarist for the other band. Being a Banshee changed him, I think. If you listen to their earlier music, it's kind of fake. Like he didn't know who he was. She opened his eyes. And now just listen, Oscar. Just listen."

I did. It was otherworldly, beautiful, haunting.

Smith started singing "Why Can't I Be You?" and Ariel, who had been sitting cross-legged on the floor, couldn't contain himself anymore. He leapt up and started to dance, his limbs lithe and balletic even amid all the frenzied post-punk moves.

I watched him, spellbound. His eyes caught mine, and he laughed, pulling me to my feet against my will.

I was a rocker. We don't dance.

But I did. I danced with absolute abandon, laughing at the joy of it.

We fell back on his bed, breathless, as slower songs followed. He talked to me about the lyrics, about the band's journey, the other groups I'd never heard of whose influences he swore he could distinguish.

"I play the guitar," I said out of the blue. "Javi, Luis, and me, we're trying to start a band."

Ariel propped his head on his palm as he turned to look at me.

"What kind of music?"

I tried not to notice the feel of his breath on my arm.

"Don't know yet. Rock, definitely. Metal, we've been thinking. But this . . ."

He laid his other hand on my arm.

"I know! I'm going to record you a mixtape, Oscar. Only the very best from my carefully curated collection. I am certain you'll find inspiration."

"Órale," I said. "And I'll show you the ropes at PSJA High School. I, uh, used to get bullied a lot, but I've figured out how to navigate the bola de rancheros there."

"We'll be each other's guides, then," he said, and there was something in his voice that made my pulse quicken.

As I had imagined, the usual suspects had all kinds of nicknames for Ariel. None were quite as creative as güero cacahuatero and mariposón, as I had been dubbed by the wannabe gangsters. But I took Ariel to our counselor, Ms. Simpson, and helped him get the same schedule as Javi and me. Since he lived in government housing like I did, we rode the same bus, listening to music on his Walkman.

For a few weeks, life in those shitty apartments was actually a delight. Mom still worked her two jobs, Fernando still spent all his time across the breezeway with Speedy Espericueta, playing Super Mario Bros. on Speedy's NES. But instead of stewing in my room alone, reading the bleak German and Russian novels that had been keeping me company in the depths of my depression, I now had a fellow freak to help while the hours away. Unabashedly, I spent time every afternoon with my new friend.

When I wasn't hanging out with Ariel, listening to his amazing collection of LPs and reading the darker of the DC comics, I was up in my apartment, learning to play post-punk songs on my battered, knockoff Fender. Javi and Luis still came to visit on the weekends, but the dynamic had changed. I could see that Ariel's presence disconcerted them.

"Is there anything you want to tell us, dude?" Javi asked one night when we got on the phone together using two-way calling.

"About?"

Luis cleared his throat. "You and Ariel, Oscar. Feels weird, the way you keep shutting us out. We figure . . . maybe you like him. As, uh, more than a friend."

"What?" I said, getting indignant to cover the panic welling up in my chest. How could they see through me like this? Was I that obvious to everyone? "Y'all never change. Always with your snide little comments about my clothes and hair."

"No, Oscar," Javi broke in. "That's not it. Yeah, we've teased you, but if you really like him, that's cool with us, carnal."

"Whatever. Pinches rancheros. You just can't handle a cool gothic kid from California."

They hung up on me. I deserved it, I guess. But I couldn't be honest with them. Better to pretend our little clique was being broken up by Ariel.

I wasn't about to exclude him.

I was growing to need him.

After Ariel's third week in Pharr, I grabbed my guitar and my sputtering amp and headed downstairs. As if he could sense me at the door, he opened before I knocked.

"¿Y esto?" he asked. "Are you planning to serenade me, Oscar Garza?"

I could feel my pale skin blushing beet red. "I just wanted to show you," I said. "I learned it."

"What?"

Before I could stop myself, I blurted, "Our song."

Pausing only briefly, he gave me a sweet smile.

"Come in, then. This calls for something special."

I went into his room and plugged in my guitar, sitting on the edge of his bed. He pulled the curtains closed and snapped a steel lighter open. I'd of course noticed the candles on his shelves before, but now he lit them, along with a stick of incense.

"Open your chakras, Oscar," he said, giving a soft laugh. "Let the music flow from the All."

Shaking my head and chuckling, I checked the tuning of my guitar and started to play. I'd slowed the tempo down and lowered the key to match my baritone better.

I couldn't bring myself to look him in the eye as I sang.

> Everything you do is irresistible
> Everything you do is simply kissable
> Why can't I be you?

I didn't even finish the song before Ariel stopped my hands on the strings, kneeling in front of me. His face was so close to mine, those lips that seemed to smile only for me, tears trembling in his eyes.

It had been months since my last kiss, back before Diana Alaniz had broken up with me.

And I had never kissed a boy before.

But I felt safe, safer than ever in my life.

I leaned forward and pressed my mouth to his. Sweet and warm, like mango just plucked from a tree.

We took our time, savoring that taste.

Over dinner that evening, my mother shared some gossip she'd heard at work.

"There's this drama teacher," she said. "From Mission or McAllen or somewhere. He's gone missing."

Fernando shrugged. "One less teacher in the world? I'm not gonna cry."

"Nando!" she scolded. "That's a terrible thing to say. But you're not letting me finish. They say he has the AIDS. That he's a homosexual and kept meeting his lovers even though he knew he could get them sick too."

I set my glass down, fuming in irritation. My mother was super religious. Ever since my uncle Samuel had come out of the closet back in 1980, she never missed an opportunity to mention how sinful his lifestyle was, how dangerous promiscuity could be, with AIDS and all the other "venereal diseases" that she liked to list like some sort of weird Rosary.

"Mom, we really don't want to hear this crap."

"Hey, some respect!" She glared at me. I already knew I reminded her of my deadbeat dad, the man she'd just divorced for abandonment. Every time I failed to live up to her expectations, she accused me of being just like him. "Anyway, they're saying that his lovers found out and came up with a plan to kidnap him."

Fernando looked at me, one eyebrow raised. "Mom watches too many telenovelas."

"I have no time for soap operas, Fernando Tomás Garza! I work myself to the bone long hours every day because your father ran off on us. So you boys just stay away from such sinful stuff, do you hear? Don't make me worry any more than I already do about you two being here alone."

I gave her a thumbs-up. "You bet, Mom. It's all copacetic."

It was her favorite word. Like a magic spell, it always calmed her down.

She crossed herself and kept eating.

After dinner, Ariel and I chatted on the phone for a while. He kept making vague references to our kiss. Part of me wanted to flirt too, but I couldn't stop thinking about the missing teacher. Couldn't get my mother's stupid voice out of my head. So I told Ariel the gossip.

"Of course it's a teacher," he grumbled. "Sleeping around like a slut. That's not what it's about, Oscar."

"No?" I said, though I had strong feelings about being faithful. I'd had several girlfriends since junior high and had never cheated on any of them.

"No. It's about following our hearts. When your heart is drawn to someone, how can you give it to another? Or your lips? Or your body?"

For a moment I imagined him, elegant and beautiful, unbuttoning his shirt . . .

"You're right. It's just a sore subject in my stupid family. My uncle's gay, and the rest of them, well, you know how Mexican men are about that shit."

There was silence on the other end. Then: "Yes, Oscar. I'm very acquainted with it. My dad beat me enough times. I don't think I'll ever forget how Mexican men are toward folks like us."

Folks like us.

My stomach flip-flopped. What was I? What was I doing with this boy?

Why now? What was it about Ariel Ortega that made me risk discovery?

"Oscar? Say something."

"Ah, Ariel. I've, uh, I've got to hit the sack."

"There's no school tomorrow, sweet boy. It's a holiday. But okay. Get your rest. Maybe we can hang out in the afternoon, yeah?"

I swallowed heavily, my mind a jumble. "Yeah. Sure we can."

"There's a dead body by the canal."

I glanced up at Fernando. A couple of hours ago I had let him go across the breezeway to Speedy Espericueta's apartment, just to get him out of my hair. Since there was no school, I was stuck baby-sitting an eleven-year-old who relished getting himself in trouble.

Now here he was, sweaty and out of breath, feeding me a ridiculous line of crap.

"Nando, what the hell, man? I told you not to leave the complex. Mom'll kill me if she knows you went to the canal again."

"Did you hear me? There's a body there, Oscar. A dead one."

"Yeah, sure there is. Why don't you take a shower or something? You stink."

He shut the door and walked over to the sofa. I dog-eared my book and really looked at him. There was fear in his eyes, genuine horror like I hadn't seen him show since Dad left.

"Dude," Fernando said, his voice hoarse, quavering, "I'm not messing with you. We went down to go fishing, me and Speedy. Then we saw them—a guy's legs, sticking out of the weeds."

That final detail convinced me. Trying to stay calm, I grabbed the phone and dialed 911. I rattled off a summary of the situation, and the dispatcher said the Pharr PD would send someone by.

There was no way I was going to let the cops show up at this government housing complex, full of all sorts of marginalized people and criminals.

"I'm calling from a pay phone. We'll meet you at the canal," I said, hanging up.

Fernando looked at me, dumbfounded. "You don't have a car."

"Yeah, but Ariel's mother does. Come on."

"We shouldn't call Mom?" Fernando asked.

"No. Last thing she needs is more stress. Don't want her freaking out and leaving work. She'd probably call in sick at the other job too."

We need to get out of this place, I didn't say. And for that we need every dime she can scrape together.

My little brother just shrugged and went downstairs with me. I'd pretty much been his surrogate dad for the past four years, and though he preferred to act all independent, he tended to follow my lead.

A single knock was all it took. Ariel opened immediately.

"Can your mom drive us to the Ridge Road canal? My little brother thinks he saw a dead body. We're supposed to meet the police there."

Gloria Ortega was shocked, but she agreed. Fernando climbed into the passenger seat. Ariel and I got in the back.

As we drove away, I glanced at the block of Section 8 apartments, the last refuge of the disposed and discarded.

That's what we are, I thought as my eyes drifted over the motley assortment of clunkers in the pitted parking lot. Discarded. Left behind.

My heart was heavy. As if sensing my spiraling emotions, Ariel reached out and took my hand. I both wanted to lace my fingers with his and to pull away; I did neither. I just let him cradle my hand like a baby as Nando guided Gloria down to Ridge Road and up the dirt path that led to the canal.

"There it is!" my brother finally shouted. The old sedan bumped to a stop, and the four of us got out. The lingering heat of early fall made everything hazy, bled color from the vegetation, leaving the meager brush pallid and dead. The hollow whine of cicadas drowned out all other noise—an ominous, predatory rattle. I wiped sweat from my face and followed Nando as he took a few hesitant steps away from the car. Behind me came Ariel and his mother, dead weeds crunching underfoot. For a moment my eyes were overwhelmed by the dusty brightness, but I squinted painfully as my little brother froze up.

And then I saw it.

Thrusting out dumbly onto the hard-packed gravel were two lifeless legs: pale, thin, coated with wiry black hair. One foot was covered by a black nylon sock; the other was bare, and I noticed with a strange sort of nausea that the man had not clipped his toenails in some time.

Gloria gasped, hurrying to pull Fernando back. Ariel came to a stop beside me, his shoulder touching mine.

Trembling, he gave whispered voice to my thoughts.

"It's him. The teacher."

A squad car pulled up. I could sense Gloria guiding my brother toward the officer who emerged, calling out to us. She must have spoken to him, but I couldn't be sure. As if from a great distance, I heard the officer call for an ambulance and backup. The dull hum of the cicadas filled my ears, thrummed in my skull like the low growl of some unseen machinery or massive beast.

I took another step. Ariel—arm around me, trying to hold me back, but I pulled away. I walked closer to the body until I could see more of him, nearly all of his torso. He was wearing black briefs and a white undershirt. Sickly weeds obscured his arms; his face was covered by the low, knotty branches of some thorny bush.

This is death. Abrupt. Meaningless. Dumb. A body, discarded, swallowed by the gaping jaws of the world. This is what they do to "folks like us," Ariel.

With a superhuman effort, I turned my back on the body.

Tears were streaming down Ariel's beautiful face. I wanted to hold him, wanted him to hold me, wanted to collapse into an embrace that would blot out the world so that only he and I remained.

But we couldn't, could we? The world was watching, ravenous, ready to devour us.

There was no hiding from those predatory eyes.

My heart broke as I pushed past Ariel and stood beside my little brother. I avoided Gloria's eyes, her questions. In a few minutes the area was swarming with cops and EMTs.

The first officer to arrive—Acosta—let us sit in the back of his patrol car. Gloria drove her weeping son away.

Once detectives were on the scene, Officer Acosta took us back to the projects, jotted down Nando's statement.

Then he drove away, and that was that.

Ariel and I didn't speak again.

Only a few weeks later, Linda Pompa became my "beard." She was a rocker girl at PSJA High School. One of her teeth was rimmed in gold, she loved Joan Jett, and she had been trying to get me to go out with her since Diana had dumped me in front of the auditorium last school year. I asked her to be my girlfriend, started walking her to class. Made out with her behind the choir room.

Ariel watched from afar, eyes red with weeping, until one day he didn't anymore.

I came home to find that he and his mother had moved away. Back to California, I supposed, or maybe another small town beyond the clutches of his abusive father.

I broke up with Linda immediately. My heart wasn't hers.

For months afterward I couldn't sleep. I would close my eyes and see those legs, that dusty, weed-entangled torso.

Every night, the body would shudder and sit up.

I wish I could tell you that it was a zombie, hungering for my flesh. . . .

But it had the face of my beloved, eyes full of tears.

Beautiful flesh covered in gaping wounds.

Lying there in my mind, discarded and decaying.

I was trapped in the weeds of my cowardice, watching his features fade from my memory into silent oblivion.

To keep the undead shell of that love alive, I slowly fed it my soul.

Late one night, a week before graduation, the phone rang. I could hear Robert Smith crooning "Torture" in the background.

"Ariel?" I asked.

There was a sob.

"Don't hang up, please," I begged, my chest aching. "I . . . I'm so sorry."

He cleared his throat. "You hurt me, Oscar. Bad."

Clenching my free hand into a fist, I nodded though he couldn't see me. "I was afraid to risk your life. Afraid to risk mine. As much as I wish I could, I can't be you. I'm not brave enough. Not strong enough."

Ariel sighed. "One day, Oscar. One day you'll find the strength. The world will change, sweet boy. Hang in there."

The line went dead. I hit *69 to call him back, but I got a busy signal.

Ariel had left my life forever.

But his words echoed in my heart. The nightmares ended. Not quite two years later, at UT Pan American, surrounded by other queer kids, I gathered the courage to be who I am.

And I fell in love with a boy again.

THE BOO HAG

UGUST IS THE WORST MONTH OF SUMMER.
When I was a boy, my granddaddy explained its horror with his Gullah wisdom: "July be sunhot, for sure, but August month? Like yesterday dinner. Us think us through with him, but him stick around and dew the grass and mold the corn and heavy the air so much the lightning bugs start a-panting."

That dog day craze lights up the face of the man who bursts into my shop, rushing up to the counter where I stand over mortar and pestle.

"Dr. Crow," he says, terror in his eyes, "Boo hag coming to get me."

I pause my grinding and peer over the rims of my cobalt-blue shades. "A boo hag. You sure?"

"Yaas," he drawls in the Gullah way. "I seen her, all dripping red and then wearing a skin what she stole. I need your help, Dr. Crow. Get rid of this haint before she kill me!"

I take a moment to size John Wilson up. He's about half a foot shorter than me, maybe thirty-five, clothes wrinkled, smell of sweat and marsh strong on him. His fear is real, nigh-on palpable. I push my shades up my nose and regard him closer through the fixed-up lenses. His soul is stained and ravaged with nefarious deeds, and death is blackly edging in.

Intrigued and concerned, I give a quick nod.

"Alright. Flip the sign on my door to closed, Mr. Wilson, and follow me."

I lay a rag over the mortar and pestle as he moves to obey, then roll the sleeves of my shirt down over the scarification on my forearms and slip my suit coat back on. Dropping my black hat atop my age-rimed twists, I lead the way.

The back room of my shop is lined with high shelves, stuffed full of mason jars and sweetgrass baskets containing the accoutrements of my trade. Some of the more dangerous things are locked away in hex-carved cabinets. There's a rickety old desk there in the middle where I do what research and figures as need doing. Nearby I've set up a cot and an old record player.

Not much else I need beyond my own aging bones.

"Sit down," I tell him as he wanders in, staring all dumbfounded at my herbs and implements. He scrapes a metal folding chair closer as I drop into my own, the cracked leather sighing like it's been hankering for my tall, thin body.

"Thankee," he breathes, running his left hand over his face. I notice the fading mark of a wedding band. "My mama sister, she say I need me a root doctor. Now, even a fool like me know you the most respected hoodoo man on St. Helena. Hell, ain't nobody better in the whole Lowcountry or all the Carolinas, even."

"Don't sweetmouth me, Mr. Wilson. I know what I am. Just give me the story, all of it."

He twitches, a mite nervous at my tone. "Yaas, sir. So, lucky me, I got me a right fine gal, clean skin and pretty. Maybe six week back, my gal, she start complain about her bones been achy and she feel tired ever morning, though she sleep sound since dark the light. Once, I wake up long after middle-night and find this horrible haint a-crouch on my gal chest, like a scrawny-ass woman except no skin:

all red meat and thick ropy veins pulsing blue. Mama learned me about boo hags when I's a child, so I reckoned I's looking upon one. Riding, like the old folk say. That hag was leaning real close, sucking up the air what come out my gal mouth."

"Her juju."

Wilson blinks, surprised by the interruption.

"It was feeding off her juju. All that's holy inside her."

He swallows, grimaces, says nothing.

I make an irritated gesture. "Go on. Crack your teeth. It'll take forever if you go all silent after every damn comment I make."

"Alright, sorry. And me, I couldn't move a muscle. Like I's jinxed, understand. Hag look at me, snarl, keep on … sucking on my gal juju. For hours, Dr. Crow. Then, just before fowl-crow, it up and fly away."

I stroke the bronzed crow skull on my necklace thoughtfully. "And what did you do?"

"Oh, I got me down to the Sherman-Williams, had them boys mix me up some haint blue for paint my gal porch and window frame. But that shit don't work, Dr. Crow. Didn't protect a damn thing."

Half-closing my eyes in annoyance, I shake my head. "Son, the Sherman-Williams employees don't know shit about haint blue. They just sold your ass some knock-off shade of indigo. Wasted your money."

"Goddamnit," he mutters. "Sumbitches. Anyways. I tried to protect her, but that boo hag come back, and this time she stole my gal away. Drug her right out the door, into the night. I reckoned she's dead, and next day I's prepare myself for tell the police or somebody, when I cold seen her walking down Sea Island Parkway, like nothing happen. Only, it wasn't my gal, you see. Not as tall, skin all baggy like if it didn't fit her good. Look right at me as I pass in my old car. She smile with teeth what ain't my gal teeth, eyes what ain't hers, neither. And ever couple days? I see her again, elsewheres. Like she stalking me. Each time a little closer to my house. I steered clear of her place, case she try and kill me. Then this morning, just past day-clean, I step onto my porch, and there she was—standing on the other side of the street, staring at me. I like to shit my pants when she start to cackle, like a crazy-ass witch from hell. Then she like make a sign…ah, can't bring the word right now. Nasty too much."

"Okay," I say, drumming my fingers briskly on the desk. "Here's what you're going to do, Mr. Wilson. I want you to go down to Cootah Flea Market, out there where you live, close to Hunting Island. You know the place. Old Mo Frederick, he's got a booth there, and he'll sell you some genuine haint blue. Get your porch roof and window trim painted. Then put your broom and a strainer, if you've got one, on either side of your bedroom door. If the hag gets in, she'll have to stop and count the straws and holes, and we can do what needs doing when she's thusly occupied."

Wilson's face lights up. "So you coming to rid me of the haint?"

"I'll show up when the sun gets red for going down. Got a few tricks up my sleeve, as you can imagine. Cost you a hundred bucks, though."

Reaching into his trousers, he pulls out a couple of wrinkled twenties. "I can get you the rest at the house, Dr. Crow. That alright?"

We shake hands, and he hurries out to take care of his part. I sit in the gloom for a few minutes, thinking. Then I pull out an old, battered flip-phone from my coat pocket.

I've got the Frogmore PD saved to my contacts. A dispatcher or receptionist or somesuch answers. A woman. I ask to speak to Detective James Barnwell. She connects me.

"Detective Barnwell."

"Mr. Bailey! I'd recognize that creepy-ass voice anywhere."

"Detective, please. Mr. Bailey was my father. If you can't bring yourself to call me Dr. Crow, Kenneth will do just fine."

We've had this conversation several times. Brother's okay, just a little too hipster for my taste. Thinks he's funny, too.

"Okay, Kenneth, what can I do for you?"

"Well, I'm going to mention a name, and I suspect you'll recognize it right off. Hoping you can give me the lowdown on him."

"Maybe. Who's the dude?"

"John Wilson. Geechee. Lives down almost to Land's End, near the marshes."

There's a choking sound, like the detective is taking a sip of something when I startle him with the name. "Oh, yeah. I know him, alright. Mechanic. Long history of domestic violence. Neighbors used to call us up all the time about him whaling away on his wife."

The tense gets my attention. "Used to."

"Yes, well, Merlene Wilson went missing three months ago, Kenneth. John claims she ran off with some fellow but can't give us any details. He's definitely a person of interest. No evidence, though. If he did it, he covered his tracks really well. Did he, uh, use hoodoo or something?"

"Nah, this fool wouldn't know rootwork if it bit him in the ass. Says he's got an unwelcome visitor."

After an uncomfortable silence, Barnwell mutters, "A haint?"

"Yup. Boo hag."

"Shit, Kenneth, weren't you bragging about how you'd rid St. Helena Island of boo hags, how they all had to go ride the poor sons of bitches up in Charleston for their juju now?"

"Yeah, well, I'm pretty certain this is a new one, Detective. Just a few months undead."

I can almost hear him thinking. "I see. So, you got this, then? I'm expecting justice all around, Dr. Crow."

That's how I know he's serious. Giving me his tacit approval. Don't need it, but it's good to know a lawman trusts the rootworker.

"It's coming, friend. I'll make damn sure."

Except for the fresh blue paint daubed here and there, John Wilson's old house has been scoured down to bare, cracked clapboards by salty winds. The tang of the marsh fills the steamy summer air, and I wish for a moment I weren't about such dark deeds this evening. Would be lovely to sit on his porch, drink some whiskey, watch the red sun die out there beyond Savannah.

He lets me in, his eyes jerking nervously across the darkening horizon before he shuts the door. I take in the simple parlor, which opens onto a kitchen on the one side. A hall appears to lead past a bathroom and guest room to a master bedroom at the end. Wilson's set up the broom and a sieve on either side of the door.

Though he's scraped away and redecorated the place, putting up a flat screen and some generic prints, I glimpse the ghostly traces of a woman's touch. Curtains. Wallpaper in the kitchen. Walking through the house, I sense Merlene Wilson everywhere. This was her home. She spent long, lonely hours making it hers.

Wilson calls me back to the kitchen.

"Swung by my mama sister house. She made Frogmore stew for me. Want some?"

"I could eat, sure."

We sit across a small dining table from each other, peeling shrimp and drinking beer as night falls outside. It's hard to gauge a man's heart, so I probe a bit.

"Your gal fix this place up before she was taken?"

His hand quivers halfway to his mouth. "Uh, no, sir. Had me a wife, once. Run off."

I raise an eyebrow. "That so? She catch you with the other woman, or did she find herself a man more to her liking?"

Anger flashes in his eyes as he clenches up his jaw. Haints scare him, but he's quick to take umbrage. If I weren't a hoodoo man, he'd probably come at me. Younger, heavier.

But he leans back, wipes his hands on a paper towel, takes a deep breath.

"Dr. Crow, you know how it be. Man gets him a lawful lady for she can give him sons, keep his house clean, make him feel a little important. Sometimes, though, a woman racktify in the head, get to thinking there more to things than that. Decide she ain't ready for no children. Start to long-eye all she ain't got. Mess up a marriage. Then one day among all, she figure she going to make a change."

I take another sip of beer. "There are men as wouldn't allow that from their wives."

"No, I reckon not. Most of us wouldn't. Most of us, we try and put them in they place."

"Like you tried to."

His eyes sort of glaze over with a mixture of hate and memory. "And failed. Had us a right ugly quarrel. She run off with some jackass. Ain't seen her since."

"And now, to add insult to injury, your gal's been killed by a haint that's wearing her skin. Can't catch a break, huh? Alright. We're going to sort this out, Mr. Wilson." I pull a vial from my shirt pocket, grab his beer bottle, sift some of the powder in.

"What you doing, Dr. Crow?"

"Well, I need you to go to sleep as soon as you can so we lure the boo hag in. But right now? You're a bundle of frantic nerves. You'll just lay in your bed, tossing and turning. This'll let you relax quicker, send you right into the Sandman's arms."

He reaches for the beer, cocks his head thoughtfully. "Where you going to be?"

"Sitting in a corner of your room. I'll darkle the air around me, deepen the shadows so she can't see me if she makes it past the wards. Once she's inside, the end will come soon."

Wilson takes a deep draught, wipes his mouth with the back of his hand. "At last, I'm a be at peace."

"Yes," I agree darkly. "Yes, you will."

It's just after midnight. Wilson is snoring lightly in his bed. I've fallen into a sort of trance, slumped in the kitchen chair I dragged to his room. The violence perpetrated in this house can't be scrubbed out like the bloodstains were. I take it all in, let it leech my compassion away.

There comes a sound like wind creaking in the eaves. Windows rattle lightly. Something inhuman scratches at the clapboards, seeking purchase. Wood groans, splinters.

As the temperature begins to rise, I hear footsteps coming down the hall, light wet slaps against the floorboards. A gagging stench of rotten meat and scarlet swamp hibiscus floods the room as the movement stops just outside the open door.

She giggles then, a childlike chuckle that deepens into spine-tingling laughter, gleeful and mad and hungry for death.

Then the boo hag bursts into the room, carrying the broom in one hand and the colander in the other. Stripped of skin, her muscles gleam slick and red in the moonlight that spills through the window. Pulsing blue like unspeakable alien tendrils, thick ropey veins crisscross her flayed flesh. Her breasts and hips are marbled white, and her ivory teeth snaggle fierce as she snarls.

With a growl, the boo hag leaps onto the bed, hunkering down on the chest of John Wilson, whose eyes flutter open and look upon her in utter horror.

"This my broom!" the haint rasps at him, enraged. "My sieve! Done counted these straws and holes before, you bastard! Day after day, cleaning and cooking for your dumb ass!"

The last shred of uncertainty unravels in my heart. This is Merlene Wilson. Her husband beat her to death in this very room, and then he dumped her corpse without ceremony into the marsh. Her soul moved on, but her spirit remained, twisted, within the shell of her body until she rose from that watery grave, transformed into a boo hag.

Undead. Hungry for juju and vengeance.

Merlene leans close to her husband's face, begins to inhale. Through my cobalt shades, I see flecks of his rotten soul drawn from between his lips into her deadly grin. Transfixed by her power, all he can do is roll his eyes in my direction and hoarsely croak my name.

"Doctor Crow!"

The boo hag snaps her head around. I shrug off the spell, let myself be seen.

"John Wilson," I say, "I only break jinxes for the innocent. The guilty? I let them suffer the consequence of their own misdeeds. You killed your wife, you goddamn fiend. I ain't lifting a hand to stop her if she wants to get her revenge."

The boo hag flings away broom and strainer, clamps her bloody hands around his throat. As she strangles him, she sucks what little holiness she can salvage from his murderous heart.

When he's dead, I stand, picking up a jar of salt from beside the chair. Merlene scrambles from the bed, regards me warily.

"The bastard deserved what he got, that's for true. You were justified." I brandish the salt, and she cringes a bit before recovering and standing defiant. "But know this—now you better get the hell off my island, Merlene Wilson. Don't want to hear a single report of sleep disturbed by a visit from you. Find your kind elsewhere or let yourself slip from that undead flesh, one of the two. Because if I run into you again here on St. Helena, I will shred your spirit to ruination with salt and hoodoo and every scrap of my considerable mojo. You understand me?"

The boo hag inclines her head ever so slightly before rushing like the night wind from that room, that house, that swamp.

I walk over to the bed, reach for Wilson's wallet on the night stand. Inside are bills. I take sixty bucks.

"Payment for services rendered, asshole," I mutter. "She won't be bothering you again."

Outside, the palmetto moon, ever watchful, shines down on me through the thick August air.

I pause on the porch for a moment, returning its baleful gaze. Then I leave, pushing my way through the dewy reeds as lightning bugs struggle to mirror that silver light.

My passing seems to snuff them out.

EL SOMBRERÓN

THE LATE AFTERNOON SUN SILHOUETTED THE TEEN AS she walked into the shelter at Sacred Heart Catholic Church late. Pulling her eyes from the distressing news about the 2016 presidential campaign that scrolled across her phone, Sister Ana Lozano smiled and stood. Other nuns, volunteers, and Jesuit priests joined her, applauding and welcoming the new arrival. But the young woman barely registered the cheerful reception, and when Sister Ana drew close, she held out her temporary papers from Customs and Border Protection without a word, staring into space with hollow eyes.

"Okay, Luisa," the nun said kindly, referring to the wrinkled sheets to glean the girl's name. "Let's get you a quick shower and some dinner. You can rest for a while, too. Then we'll talk about what comes next."

Most of the refugees emerged refreshed and renewed after a few minutes beneath the warm spray of water, dressed in gently used clothes. However, Luisa Orellana still appeared numb to the world, glancing about with harrowed expectation as she sipped some broth and bit reflexively into a slice of bread.

After she had eaten, Sister Ana guided her to a cot, where she sat listlessly for a while, refusing to lie back, until startled, not by any of the loud bustling of others, but by the soft instrumental guitar music that drifted from some volunteer's phone.

"Could you," she whispered hoarsely, "turn that off?"

Accustomed to the unusual requests of people at their wits' end, Sister Ana complied with a smile, apologizing to the owner.

Picking up a brush, she returned to her charge. "Do you mind if I help you with your hair, Luisa? We can chat a bit, discuss your plans and options."

Luisa nodded, though she winced when the nun's fingers touched her long, beautiful hair.

"So," Ana began, slowly pulling the brush down that cascade of black, "you're from Guatemala, aren't you? Do you have relatives in the US?"

"Yes. My aunt. She lives in Chicago."

"Are you going to wait for other family members before heading that way?" This was often the case with the refugees. They arrived singly or in pairs, joining up in McAllen for the final leg of their trek.

"No. I'm alone. No one else is coming."

Sister Ana drew a sharp breath despite herself. She had heard so many horror stories about the military and the maras that she simply assumed the worst. But Luisa's head twisted slightly beneath her palms.

"They're not dead if that's what you're thinking. When I left, everyone was fine. We live in a highland village, close to Lake Atitlán. We're farmers, and life is pretty peaceful there. Sometimes the guerrilla or a hurricane comes smashing into the mountains, but mostly we are left alone with the jungle, the sky and the xocomil winds that sweep off the lake to purify our sins."

She fell silent for a time. Ana knew better than to press. The teen would tell what she needed to tell when she was ready to tell it. No use asking too many questions.

After a few more strokes of the brush, Luisa continued her tale.

"It was about a year ago when we found the first burro with its mane carefully plaited in small, smooth braids. Everyone knew what this meant. Word spread throughout the entire village, and every unmarried girl or woman age ten or older was given a curfew by the council of elders."

Luisa turned her face a bit to look askance into the nun's eyes.

"It was el Sombrerón. He had come out of the jungle, looking for a bride."

Unbidden, a shiver uncoiled itself along Ana's spine. She had heard whispered mentions of that ancient goblin from other Central Americans who had passed through Sacred Heart. Short, barefoot, face obscured by a wide-brimmed hat, the creature at times ventured from his shadowy home, a guitar strung across his back. Some evenings, legends said, he would lead a pack of mules through a town, hoping to encounter a girl to enchant with his song. If he succeeded, he would ask to braid her hair.

Once his fingers snarled their way through those tresses, the girl would be his forever.

Forcing her hands to stop trembling, Sister Ana continued the grooming, chiding herself for being foolish enough to let the folklore of a distant land affect her so. As the sun began to set, she kissed her crucifix and said a silent prayer of thanks for her own blessings.

"I was always too independent, my mother used to tell me," Luisa mused wistfully. "Reluctant to obey tradition or accept the guidance of adults. So one night I decided to slip out and sit beneath my favorite tree, staring at the stars and imagining some different destiny.

"Then I heard the music. The plucked and strummed strings of an old guitar, shimmering and bright like the moonlight. And a voice so pure and lovely that I at first thought some angel had descended from heaven to visit me. When he stepped out of the shadows, though, I saw how wrong I was. It was el Sombrerón, wearing his patchwork clothes and smiling wickedly beneath the brim of a hat that made him seem even smaller and more impish. I wanted to run, but I was frozen in place by the music. He crooned to me sweetly, promising so many things—long life and beauty and adventure. All I had to do was let him braid my hair. 'A single plait,' he sang, 'so delicate and smooth that your parents will never see it.'

"I heard my mother, then, screaming my name in desperation. The spell was broken. I stood and ran back to my house, weeping. I told my parents everything, and they swore to protect me."

Luisa's eyes welled with tears. "We knew what was at stake. That single braid marks a woman as his, and though he appears to leave, he in truth lingers to feed on her despair. He sprinkles her meals with dirt and pebbles till she refuses to eat, wasting away from lack of food and a longing for his lovely voice, his deft little hands. Some survive his torture, but they age much too fast and spend the remainder of their days old and alone, untouched by any love beyond the memory of his songs."

The teen's hair had now dried and hung in a dark, luxurious sheet down her bent back.

"I tried to hide. But he returned again and again, and his song was harder and harder to resist. Finally I left without a word, crossing into Mexico and riding la Bestia, that horrible old train, across thousands of kilometers—beaten and mistreated by some, protected and helped by others—just to escape the goblin's grasp."

There was bleak silence for a moment as the implications of her flight curdled in the nun's ears, almost making her shudder.

She shrugs off physical abuse as if it's nothing compared to the darkness she fears. Is it trauma? Is this how she copes, creating a monster to explain away the nightmare she's faced?

Sister Ana finally spoke, keeping her doubts about the story to herself. "Well, now you're here, my dear. Now you're safe."

Notes quavered in the air. Luisa stiffened, but Ana patted the crown of her head.

"It's just that volunteer again. I'll ask him to choose some other sort of music."

She didn't get a chance to stand, however. The notes resolved into a melody, strange and ancient, beautiful beyond description. Then came the voice, soothing and seductive, intoning words in a language Ana could not hope to ever comprehend. As she listened, however, she somehow *did* catch the meaning, as if the music had sent waves of images and emotions into her very soul.

He sang of a long-forgotten time, before mankind had lifted lofty temples to the gods, unfurling cities around them. A time when the Little Folk had ruled the world, their magic untrammeled and unrivaled, faithful servants of the Feathered Serpent. Then he sang of their fall, the rise of Man, and the further descent of one rebellious band, damned and disfigured, goblins scheming in the darkness until they had forged an emissary, a seducer, an angel of death.

El Sombrerón stepped out from behind the dividing curtain, his hands caressing his guitar bewitchingly as he weaved his way through the gloaming toward them. Luisa yanked herself away from the nun, a cry choking in her throat as she stumbled away.

Sister Ana, however, was transfixed.

Let me braid your hair, the goblin whispered. A single plait. No one need ever know. I see your yearning, your long and bitter wait for a magic that will strip this empty world away. It can be yours now, Ana. Just let me touch your hair.

She neither moved nor spoke as he slid his guitar to his back and clambered onto the cot behind her. Part of her was drawn to his seduction. Part of her was struck dumb and immobile by existential fear. But more than anything, she wanted to give Luisa a fighting chance.

Run, she urged with all her soul. Take that ticket, get on the bus to Chicago. Don't look back. I'll give myself to him instead. He'll have to stay to feed on me. You'll be safe.

Humming his ancient melody, el Sombrerón unpinned her grey-streaked hair, which fell loosely to her shoulders.

Then he took up three strands and began to braid.

WHEN THE SKY FELL

QHIRTLAHIK WATCHED THE STAR STREAM toward his village.

The priest claimed stars were the Guardians of the Dark, where Mother Sun hid her face in shame for the People's sins each night. Alone out of all her feathered children she had given them souls, yet they were ungrateful. So the divine visions proclaimed.

Qhirtlahik doubted. It was his sin. He watched the skies at night, scratching the stars' paths into a wide sheet of bark with his talon.

They did a dance. More regular than the tides, than the passing of the seasons, than the coming and going of rain and heat and cool.

A week ago, he had noticed a new one, growing larger each night, defying the dance.

Now, even with the dawn claws of Mother Sun bloodying the horizon, the star would not fade. It was nearly as big as Sister Moon.

Qhirtlahik could have sworn he saw flames flickering across its widening face.

Looking down the hill at his village, he felt his feathers ripple with fear. His tongue flicked at the air, a nervous impulse.

As one of the Knowers, Qhirtlahik had traveled far from the People's cluster of villages.

Off yonder, in the Outlands, he had learned a sobering truth.

No other thinkers, no other speakers existed beyond their little spar of land, jutting into the Iridescent Sea.

Perhaps, he thought, *I should take my friends and flee.*

This star might consume us all. There would be no People left. No sign we were ever here. Our wattle and daub homes shattered. Reduced to ash our wooden weapons, bone tools. The sigils we score into flexible bark effaced forever.

And beyond? What survives? The lumbering monsters whose rainbow feathers mimic our own? The smaller ones, desperate to fly? The burrowers, warm-blooded and timid?

Mother Sun thrust her face into the sky.

The falling star outshone her.

THROWING BONES

THE CONCH TRUMPET SIGNALS THE THIRD WATCH OF the night when Zolli emerges from the temple into the chilly darkness. Stars glitter above the sacred district of Tenochtitlan, but the moon has not risen, so darkness is deep along the broad streets. On a normal night Zolli would feel no fear, but there are foreign troops in the city—the bearded soldiers of Caxtillan, who crossed the sea in boats like houses to invade these lands astride massive deer, their unbreakable silver armor and swords glittering vicious in the autumn sunlight of the highlands.

The men themselves are not the problem. Zolli has bedded many a warrior, and he understands how to channel their roiling passions. These pale, ugly brutes would drop to their knees before his considerable beauty and charm. No, the emperor's absence is what twists his innards with worry. The family of Lord Moctezuma continues to assure citizens that he has simply withdrawn from the world for a time, ruling in private consultation with the visiting general. No one believes this obfuscation, of course.

The Caxtiltecah have taken our sovereign hostage, and none of us is truly safe. Even the most sacred byways of the city darkle with menace.

Shuddering, Zolli draws his robes more tightly about him, hurrying west toward his clan's borough. Then, as if signaled by the young man's uneasy thoughts, a helmeted figure steps into the street before him, reeking of wine and sweat. Slurring syllables in his savage tongue, he sidles close to Zolli, pulls the young man to him. His rough hands stroke that long, braided hair, trace trembling those delicate features.

A mess, but perhaps I can learn something. Dizzy his mind, plunge him deep in a trance.

The foreigner presses his mouth against Zolli's, bites at his lips, slips his tongue past his teeth. Struggling to ignore the filthy beard, Zolli returns the kiss. The soldier's hands slide down his body, cup his buttocks, hike up his robes. A rough palm feels its way along his inner thigh, higher, higher, till it seizes his stiffening member.

Recoiling, the Caxtiltecatl shoves Zolli away. Eyes wide, the soldier spits and snarls.

"Puta malika!"

Though the words are meaningless, Zolli understands. The brute has confused him for a woman, dressed and coifed as he is. Raising a reassuring hand, the young man takes a step forward.

"Relax, friend. I am a servant of Xochipilli, Prince of Flowers. There is nothing to…"

Barking in his barbarous tongue, the soldier unsheathes his sword and buries it deep into Zolli's belly. The pain is sharp, spreading cold fire through his guts. The young man collapses, sliding off the blade. His blood pools blackly upon the road. His eyes begin to glaze.

There is a form in the darkness. White glints among the black. The form swirls out of the shadows. It appears to be a woman, wearing a red huipil blouse and skirt. Around her neck loops a chain from which small skulls dangle. Her face is obscured by the black mantle that covers her head and extends past her knees, glittering with silver stars.

She stretches forth a skeletal hand, denuded of all flesh, gripping a sickle carved from human bone in which embedded obsidian glints cruelly.

This is Mictecacihuatl, Lady Death, come to reap the young man's soul.

Nearby, flowery vines whip from a canal, webbing their way along walls and street to pool in coils beside Zolli's dying flesh. One of the buds burgeons larger and larger into a human-size pod that cracks open, revealing a beautiful youth with blossoms braided into his long hair. Bare-chested except for a collar from which hang mother-of-pearl teardrops, the god otherwise wears a simple breechclout and armbands of copper.

"Xochipilli, Prince of Flowers." Mictecacihuatl's voice is like gravel in a corpse's throat.

"Revered Lady Death," the newcomer acknowledges with a bow. "I see you've come for one of my servants."

"Yes. His life has nearly ebbed away."

The Prince of Flowers kneels beside the dying temple prostitute. "Let me take him with me. I'll infuse him with life, keep him by my side."

In Lady Death's other hand she holds an orb. It glows brighter as she lifts it, revealing the naked skull of her face. The blue flames of her eyes flare with indignation.

"No. His soul is mine."

The Prince of Flowers stands, enraged. "You cold, greedy bitch. What difference does one soul make, now? Have you seen these bastards the Lord of Chaos has dragged across the ocean? Their weapons? The diseases squirming in their unclean guts? You'll soon have millions of shades in your bony hands."

"All the same."

Sighing, Xochipilli makes a small gesture, and the vines at his feet erupt in marigolds, the favorite flower of the queen of the underworld. "Listen, it's all very fine for you. You'll probably survive the change. But for most of us, this is the end. The beauty and pleasures and knowledge that I steward are despised by this barbarous people. How long until I simply fade into the Green World? What does it cost you to grant me this final joy?"

Lady Death gives a dismissive wave of her sickle. The flowers wither. "We each of us must grapple with the consequences as best we can. You have no claim upon me, no right to bend my will to yours."

"No, of course I don't. But show mercy, Sovereign of Shades," he pleads. "Understand. I chose this boy when he was very young. As my priests shuddered in narcotic trance, calling upon me in ecstasy, I whispered his name to them, guided them to the child. He was consecrated to me in my temple, groomed to be my servant, dressed beautifully, taught the ways of pleasure. Down the years, he has shown great compassion, wisdom, skill. He is my favorite, valued above all others. I'm willing to meet whatever terms you set."

Lady Death scoffs, disgusted. "I will not barter with you, Xochipilli. To do so is beneath us both. However, I know your predilection for gambling and play. Perhaps you would agree to a game of chance."

A smile brightens the youthful face of the Prince of Flowers. "Perfect. Which did you have in mind?"

Her hands retreat into her mantle, and she draws forth a wooden board.

"Patolli, little brother. We will play patolli for the soul of your beloved."

With an impish nod, Xochipilli claps his hands, and the vines at their feet grow into a sort of living table. Mictecacihuatl sets the board down. Carved on its surface are two perpendicular paths that intersect like the axis mundi. At the crossroads are four large squares. Each of the four branches have rounded ends and are divided lengthwise and crosswise, forming sixteen spaces. The fourth and fifth rectangles on either side are further bisected into triangles.

"Okay. So we both know the rules," the Prince of Flowers said. "Each of us bets six valuable items."

Lady Death pulls a black bag from her robes. "You must offer up the six tools of your entheogenic communication with humanity. Nothing less will do."

Blanching a bit, Xochipilli groans. "Fine. Let it be noted that I stake holy mushrooms, sun-openers, tobacco blooms, the flowers of the funereal tree, the special morning glory called snake-plant and my delicate sea moonflowers. An item per marker, forfeit if I land on a triangle, all of them due you should you win the game. Content? Now, what things will you put at risk?"

She gives a raspy laugh. "Oh, I offer nothing beyond the mere life of the ephebe. As you say, the arrival of the conquerors has foreshortened your relevance considerably. I calculate you will be a viable god for another half-dozen years or so. So I agree to restore one year of existence to young Zolli every time the rules require forfeiture from me. Of course, in the unlikely event you should defeat me, his natural span will be restored. I cannot speak to how long that might be."

There is silence; then the Prince of Flowers whispers, "You are heartless."

"My function is the meting out of justice, the purification of souls. Compassion is superfluous. Now, do you agree to my terms?"

"Yes, I agree to your damn terms." His eyes flash with resigned humor. "Luck may be on my side tonight. We'll see."

Lady Death shakes items from her bag. Twelve pieces of jade, six red and six green. Xochipilli claims the latter. "Clearly red is your color," he quips.

Finally, five small bones clatter upon the board. Each has been painted with a dot of blood on one side.

"Ah, so we've dispensed with the traditional red beans and white spots. Let me guess—the fingers of children? You are nothing if not reliably morbid, Sister."

Lady Death rolls first, gets a single dot on her first throw, allowing her to place a marker at the center of the board on one of the larger squares. Xochipilli rolls a four, a two, a five. His opponent has three pieces in play before the bones come up with just the one red-brown smear, permitting him to actually begin.

She consistently rolls high, three or four and often five, that unlikely outcome that gives a player double the moves. Two of her pieces have finished the entire circuit of spaces without landing on triangles before Xochipilli even has all six bits of green jade on the board. The bones he throws give him smaller advances, send him skipping again and again into forfeiture. His psychotropic plants are lost to him one by one, and with them his ability to shape lives.

There are five pieces on the board—one of hers, four of his—when the Prince of Flowers groans and raises a hand. "It's all this playing with baby phalanges that's ruining my luck. Can't we switch to beans or morning glory seeds or something?"

"No."

Xochipilli looks over at the blue-tinged form of the human youth. His heart aches with sadness and loss. In desperation, he considers cheating, reaching through the vines into the wood of the game board, making it tremble at just the right moment so that Lady Death must forfeit at least one year. But she will know, and all will be for naught.

There is only one chance, a once-in-a-lifetime stroke of luck built into the rules that can turn the entire game on its head.

Closing his eyes, Xochipilli reaches out through the cosmos, searching for a familiar fire, the mischievous dancing energy of Old Coyote, his first and best lover, gender-shifting god of good fortune.

Please, Huehuecoyotl. For all those trysts among desert hoodoos, unbridled passion beneath the pulsing Milky Way. Smile on me but a moment. Give me my heart's desire.

"I believe it is your turn, little brother," Mictecacihuatl sneers. "Or do you yield?"

Without looking, the Prince of Flowers reaches out, seizes the bones, lifts his hand, and lets them fall.

Lady Death gives a most uncharacteristic gasp. "Impossible!"

Slowly, Xochipilli opens his eyes. The fingers are all standing on edge, neither their blank nor marked side facing upward.

"The Auspicious Throw," he shouts with glee. "All the goods are mine! Come, dear sister, declare me the winner."

Furious, she sweeps the markers and bones into her bag, thrusts the board back into her mantle. "I have no idea how you managed that, besotted child, but very well. You are the victor. The boy's life is yours. Enjoy him while it lasts."

Reaching out with her orb, she touches Zolli's forehead and whirls off, vanishing into the shadows.

Zolli feels his soul being pulled back through the gray curtain that divides the world of men from the Land of the Dead. That roiling river, that sterile sand, those stark and crashing peaks slowly fade, replaced by darkness and the familiar tang of his city's predawn air.

The young man spasms, coughs, sits up with a start, his lips parting to loose a cry.

"Shhh."

Above him looms a beautiful figure, like spring made flesh. There is no need to ask. Zolli knows his lord from countless sweet yet fleeting dreams. The Prince of Flowers kneels, takes the youth in his arms.

"But how? I was dead. I had crossed the boundary into the Place of the Shorn."

"I wagered for your life, lovely boy. Bet all that I have. And I won. But your soul, ah, that is yours alone to give."

Zolli's eyes fill with tears as he reaches up to caress that petal-strewn hair. "Foolish god," he whispers, overwhelmed with lust and love and longing, "I gave myself to you long ago."

He pulls the Prince of Flowers close, sealing his vow at last with a long and holy kiss.

As dawn bloodies the eastern skies above the trackless sea, Xochipilli enfolds himself and his lover in leaves and vines, creating a cocoon in which verdant ecstasy slows for a while the cruel march of time.

THE CHALLENGE

DURING THE WANING YEARS OF TOLTEC REIGN over Mesoamerica, the aging king of Tollan called his two sons before him. Sitting on his feathered mat upon his jade throne, he addressed them with solemn ceremony.

"You have both concluded your studies well, though it is clear that you, my elder son, have the keener reflexes, grasp of history, and mind for strategy; while you, his younger brother, show great aptitude for philosophy, music, and the oratory required of a true statesman.

"You have both furthermore demonstrated your valor in battle, slaying enemies and taking captives without fear. It is true, my younger son, that your style is foolhardier and more fluid; your elder brother instead commands the respect of his colleagues and unerringly transforms disparate warriors into a seamless fighting body, devastating to its foes.

"Hear me, my sons. I am proud of you both. I believe that under the right circumstances, either of you could rule this kingdom. But you know our ways. Each prince must prove himself worthy of the mat of authority. So today, you shall both leave my palace, set out with nothing but your breechclouts, your flesh, your minds—and you will work a mighty victory in the name of your father the king."

With a bow, the brothers quit the throne room and disappeared into the haze of a distant horizon while the city looked on in sober silence.

Months passed. The royal spies brought back fleeting rumors, but the king waited in quiet, tortured suspense for the return of his sons, praying to the twin gods of chaos and creation for their success.

An entire ceremonial year passed before heralds trumpeted on their golden conches the arrival of both princes. Their father stood in the portico of his palace and watched as from the north a phalanx of warriors approached, his elder son at their head in the regalia of a general.

Circling around the palace from the south came the younger prince, skin a darker burnished bronze but wearing the same simple breechclout as when he had left. Slung across his chest was a bag woven from reeds.

After embracing them on the steps, the king took his place upon his throne and bade them speak of their triumphs before a gathered group of courtiers, counselors, and generals.

"I traveled to the north, Your Majesty," the elder explained, "to barbarian lands. There I came across a band of Chichimec mercenaries who sought to enslave me. After I bested a dozen of their number with my bare hands, however, they allowed me to join their ranks. We fought in several battles, contracted by one desert kingdom or another, and my superior training and prowess soon garnered me a command.

"Then came the day that a client tribe refused to pay the accorded fee, and I rallied the barbarian warriors to follow me in seizing control of their lands. That people fell easily beneath our obsidian-tipped lances and mighty clubs, and I was declared leader of the hybrid nation. A fortnight ago, we began marching south toward Your Majesty's realm, and along the way we have conquered two more city-states, which I now lay at your feet, Father, as vassal nations, along with the ten thousand men in the army that I now command."

The king's normal dour expression was broken by the hint of a smile. "My son, you have more than demonstrated your worth. I accept your gift with pride and recognize you as a general of the Toltec domain."

The prince bowed low and went to stand among the other military leaders. The aging sovereign then turned his gaze upon his younger son, who came forward, forehead high, eyes gleaming with what seemed inhuman surety and peace.

"Lord Father," he began, "knowing the likely path to victory of my brother, I elected to travel south, into the highlands. There I found shamans who counseled me and bequeathed me the six holy sacraments of the Flowery God—peyote, mushrooms, morning glory seeds, tobacco leaves, moonflowers, sun-openers.

"I scaled the divine peaks of the White Mountain, struggling against the cold and snow. When I reached the summit, I prepared the narcotic concoction the ancients called *gods' gall*. Readying myself through prayer and bloodletting, I took a deep draught. A whirlwind of cosmic energy unmoored my soul from my flesh, and I found myself rising toward the sun.

"That fiery god was surprised to find me in his orbit, and he reached out to bat me away. But I seized his flaming limbs and began to grapple with him, striving to pin him to the earth or sky. Locked thus in combat, the sun and I wheeled through the heavens for many months of thirteen days, plunging each evening into the bowels of the earth, where the shades of my ancestors beheld our titanic struggle.

"Over time, I robbed the god of rest. His charring heart began to cool. And one morning, as we emerged at the horizon from the

Land of the Dead, I tumbled the sun to his distant, watery kingdom. He bowed and acknowledged defeat."

An outraged rumor rippled through the throne room. The elder son shook his head, irate and embarrassed. The nobles of the realm stiffened, anticipating judgment.

"My son," the king rasped. "Surely you know how difficult this story is to credit."

"Indeed, Your Majesty. Such was my thought when the blazing god prepared to return me to my flesh. No one will believe me."

The prince ascended the first few steps of the dais. His brother moved forward, spear in hand, ready to intercept.

"Yet hear me well, Father," the younger prince whispered. "I strove with the sun himself, and in the end, I won. As proof and tribute, I bring you a blossom, plucked from the fields of paradise that skirt the Holy House of Dawn."

He drew from his reed bag an unearthly, achingly beautiful flower and laid it at the feet of the king, its petals still glowing with ineffable light.

THE SUMMIT

THE FIRST THING WE SEE ARE HER HANDS: STRONG fingers, gloved in sky blue, clutching icy rock. She hauls herself over the jutting lip and it's clear she is a woman. Light brown skin beneath the impenetrable dark of her goggles, thin lips chapped like a fissure along her narrow jaw. The wind gusts painful against that face, yanking on her hood, making the fur lining dance almost alive in the pale afternoon sun.

From a greater distance, we watch as her body moves up the slope with nimble surety. There is an emblem on the back of her parka, the green and white of the Pakistan flag. Before we can give this revelation much thought, an updraft sends flurries swirling around her and she presses herself tight against the rock. She has no harness. No ropes or cables can save her if she falls. We question the woman's sanity for a moment, our stomachs tightening in apprehension. What could have driven her to make this deadly ascent?

Farther back. The peak looks familiar to us. We've seen it in so many documentaries, movies, photos.

Everest. Tallest mountain on our planet.

The woman clambers at last onto the final ridge and walks to the summit. For a moment she just stands there upon that snow-clogged sliver of stone 29,000 feet above sea level. Then she tilts her head back, scans the thin and misty heavens.

She is waiting for something. But the sky is empty.

Carefully, she shuffles toward the edge and peers below. We cannot see her eyes, but the emotion comes across in the stiffening of her stance, the squeezing of gloved fingers into fists.

We pull away slowly, the hollow wind keening soft around us. There is the Second Step a thousand feet below the mountaineer, and a little lower, the First Step.

Now we can see Camps V and VI, surrounded by bits of bright color standing out amid the snow. Generations of corpses lie here—frozen, gruesome landmarks.

We begin to hear something now, a strange and mangled chorus that blends with the bitter wind. Forms are stirring in the snow, struggling to rise.

Our pulses racing, we continue to retreat from this inexplicable scene, only to be faced with something even more harrowing. Some five thousand feet below our lone mountaineer, a wave of dark bodies surges up the slope, snarling and clawing at the icy rock. Emaciated men and women. Children as well. All wearing tattered clothes that cannot possibly keep them warm enough to remain among the living.

Hints of bone glint in the tenuous sunlight. One figure is missing half his face. Another trails frozen intestines that snap off beneath the blackened feet of a moaning child. Something not much more than a skeleton drags its bones in hissing rage.

All of them stare at the summit as they push ever onward, their yellowed eyes locked on the solitary woman who stands above them.

How many of these creatures are there? We zoom out, farther and farther. The horror overwhelms us.

The entire mountain is teeming with the undead, roiling and festering with raging corpses. We begin to sweep around Everest, moving from its north slope clockwise, scanning every possible ascent.

Millions upon millions of snarling zombies cover three-quarters of the mountain. Millions more are storming the Mahalangur Himal range, darkening those snowy skirts like a demonic blight.

We wonder for a moment what drives them. She is just one woman, after all. But consider their gaunt and rotted silhouettes. How long has it been since they last fed on the flesh of the living? Do hunger and the herd instinct push them to these extremes?

The harsh cacophony rising from that innumerable mass engulfs us for a moment, but then we make out, faint and stuttering, the thrumming of a helicopter.

Leaving the zombie horde behind, we spiral back up the mountain to the summit. The mountaineer has backed down to the ridge and is waving to a Bell UH-1 Huey that approaches in strange up- and downward swoops, as if its pilot were forced to find gusts of winds to stay aloft in the rarified air.

We see crossed swords, crescent moon and star—the helicopter belongs to the Pakistan Army Aviation Corps. It lowers uneasily to the summit, jerking back and forth, scraping its skids along the snow. The mountaineer, head down, hurries forward and jerks open the door, almost falling as the aircraft tilts without warning.

Then she is inside, dropping into a seat, grabbing the headset to communicate with the pilot.

"Where is it, Shambi?" Her voice is hoarse, rasping with rage and looming despair. "I thought you were going to strap it to the skids!"

The pilot, who wears a military-issue flight suit, makes a brusque gesture toward the back of the helicopter. "I had to bring it, Bibi. Threw everything off balance otherwise."

"Shit. All right."

Seizing a dangling mask and gulping at oxygen for a moment, Bibi gets back up and makes her way to the rear. All the other seats—every bit of extra weight—have been removed. She pulls a short line from her parka, clips it to her belt and to a metal loop on the hull. Then she kneels before the long heavy object that has been strapped awkwardly to the floor.

It is a nuclear warhead. She begins to arm it.

The helicopter teeters back and forth as Shambi struggles to keep control. He catches an updraft, hovers twenty feet or so above the summit.

Bibi slaps his shoulder, nods. "It's ready!" She shouts above the rotors and the wind. "I've set the timer and cut it free! But it's too heavy, Shambi!"

"Just open the door! I'll tilt us so it falls out."

Bibi nods and yanks back on the lever. The door wrenches open, and the pressure drops as the plaintive wind whips through the interior of the helicopter. She hurries to the seat and straps herself in as Shambi yaws and rolls the shuddering craft till the warhead begins to slide toward the opening.

It hits lengthwise and won't fit through. Shambi tries rolling back and forth, but the wind outside kicks up to almost 200 mph, and the two find themselves close to spinning out of control.

"Wait!" Bibi calls through the headset. "I'll get it oriented."

Gritting her teeth, she clambers to the back and anchors herself near the door. She gives Shambi a thumbs up while the wind pulls at her insistently, eager to send her plunging back to those dead-crowded slopes.

This time when the helicopter rolls, she braces herself against the hull and kicks at the warhead with a booted foot, skewing its trajectory so the bomb is at an angle when it reaches the doorway and plunges out into the air.

Bibi's strap snaps at that moment, and she goes tumbling after. Our hearts lurch with fear. Below, the zombies, perhaps sensing a reprieve for their eternal hunger, yearn toward the sky like putrid blooms.

But as she passes through the opening, the mountaineer's hand shoots out and grabs the doorframe. She dangles for a desperate moment over the abyss, three fingers supporting her weight against the ineluctable pull of gravity. With a cry, Shambi begins to right the helicopter. Bibi's feet scrabble for a breathtaking moment against the skids and then she surges inside, panting with effort and hypoxia. Crawling, she manages to slide the door shut against the tremendous gale. Then she pulls herself slowly to her seat, strapping in and donning both oxygen mask and headset.

"You okay?"

Giving an almost imperceptible shake of her head, she mutters, "I'm alive."

Ten minutes pass in relative silence as Shambi flies away, dropping in altitude while Mount Everest recedes in the distance.

"How much longer?" he finally asks.

"Any second now, little brother." Her voice is hollow, exhausted. We can only guess at the dangers she has braved, the mad desperation that sent her into the Himalayas trailing tens of millions of zombies.

There is a dull flash like muted apotheosis. In the distance, a mushroom cloud blossoms over the Mahalangur Himal. We imagine the blast, melting ice and snow, obliterating the living dead. A few seconds later, the helicopter shudders a little, relative calm compared to the turbulence the pilot faced above the summit.

"Praise God," Shambi mutters. "It worked. Now a few more hours of flight, refuel at New Delhi, and on to Shimshal."

They are low enough now that Bibi can remove the mask. She thrusts up her goggles, revealing haunted eyes brimming with tears of relief. Our own chests constrict with emotion. We do not know her, but she is precious to us now.

"Yes, back home."

Her brother says nothing for a moment, his hand tightening on the cyclic. Then he voices the fear that we have begun to contemplate as well.

"What if we didn't get them all, Bibi?"

Pulling her gloves off, she flexes those strong and skillful fingers. The narrow line of her lips twists into a grimace or smile.

"Then I'll just climb another mountain, won't I?"

EPHEMERA

I N THE THIRTY-SIXTH YEAR OF THE LONG REIGN OF EMPEROR Axayacatl, his wife Asako cajoled him into reinstating Tanabata as an imperial holiday. The Star Festival was the perfect time, she suggested, for his subjects to implore the gods for the skills they needed to maintain the glory of the Empire. Such an outpouring of dutiful verse—the traditional conduit of these special prayers—from Tenochtitlan to Kyoto would continue to cement the hegemony of Anahuac and curb any expansion by the Ming.

As fate would have it, the Imperial Poet Macuilxochi-tzin was summering in Kyoto the month of the festival, staying at the palatial estate of Ahuizotl, her second cousin and younger brother of the emperor. As tlatoani of Kyoto and more broadly shogun of the Nipponese isles, Ahuizotl saw it as his duty to blend his homeland's cultural sensibilities, toltecayotl, with the more Buddhist notion of wabi-sabi. Therefore he declared that, to conclude the festivities, the aging Mexica princess would engage in a public conversation on poetry with Sogi, beloved itinerant monk and master of the renga form of linked verse. Now in his seventy-fourth year, Sogi had taken up residence at the Shokoku-ji temple, and he expressed cheerful willingness to participate.

Preparations began a week before the festival, on the very first day of Huey Tecuilhuitl, the eighth solar month. Dew was harvested from taro leaves each morning to create a special ink. Paper merchants prepared the tanzaku strips upon which the people would write their prayer poems. Children made origami stars and cranes. Bamboo trees were trimmed.

All across the Empire of Anahuac, the subjects of Axayacatl considered their prayers carefully, composing onegaikoto in the secret recesses of their hearts, revising those syllables to meet the strictures of the waka form. In Nahuatl, Nihongo, or—in the case of many intellectuals—Guanhua, the language of the Middle Kingdom, poems lay waiting for brush and ink and paper.

The morning of Tanabata arrived. Men, women and children donned colorful garments—kosode, huipil, tilma—and committed their prayers to tanzaku, which they then hung on bamboo or ceiba trees along with the origami figures they had prepared. A million patriotic pleas, spiraling slowly into heaven, pleasing to the gods. The air was redolent with happy piety.

The streets were a riot of color—regional dances, parades, processions of the lovely impersonators of goddesses Xilonen and Cihuacoatl, whose ceremonial month it was. There was music and sport and an abundance of food; none lacked for entertainment with so many jugglers, actors, clowns.

As shadows began to lengthen across Kyoto that afternoon, hundreds were permitted to stream through the gates of the imperial compound to lounge amidst the shogun's gardens and await the unprecedented encounter.

A raised wooden platform had been erected at the foot of a bridge that spanned a koi-laden brook. Attendants busied themselves upon it, laying out mats and writing material. Then, with stately fanfare and pomp, the shogun crossed the bridge with an entourage of retainers and attendants, calling out to his people.

"Imperial subjects, welcome. During this Star Festival we celebrate unlikely connections. Tonight the gods Orihime and

Hikoboshi, separated the rest of the year by the glowing river of heaven, are reunited at last. So, too, did our two great peoples reach across the vast sea to join together as a single, mighty empire. And now, we bear witness to the very first encounter of our two greatest living poets."

From gaudy pavilions emerged the two elderly figures, making their stately way to the platform and kneeling upon the mats. Macuilxochitzin spread her jade-green cueitl skirt carefully, her bronze skin contrasting starkly with the white of her blouse and braided hair. She drew a low writing table close and glanced at Sogi, who wore the saffron yellow robe common to Buddhist priests. He winked at her. Narrowing her eyes a bit, she spoke.

"When the Emperor arrived on these isles, he found this city a smoking ruin. Both the shogun and his deputy were dead, but the civil war had spread like wildfire. Lord **Axayacatl** and his generals had soon pushed the Yamana clan onto the island of Shikoku, where definitive victory was won. I celebrated this feat in a poem twenty years ago. To honor today's festivities, I have translated part of it for you."

Drawing a deep breath, she looked down at the characters before her and began to declaim.

> Axayacatl, you tore down
> the castle of Jizogatake.
> Your flowers and your butterflies
> went spiraling through Iyo,
> Sanuki, Tosa, and Awa—

Your might gladdened our hearts
like the songs of our homeland.

Gravely you offered
flowers and plumes
to the Lord of the Near
and the Nigh.

You laid eagle shields
in God's hands
in that perilous place,
that burning plain:
the battlefield.

Like our songs,
like our flowers,
you gladden the Giver of Life,
O Master of the Sea-Ringed World.

And He who stands
forever at our side
is burgeoning
with ocean flowers, fire buds—
those blossoms of war—
blissfully intoxicated.

The Mexica princess folded her hands upon her lap. "Everyone
knows that my father was Tlacaelel, advisor to three emperors before

his death. When the Ming reached our ancestral shores, he understood the moment was divinely ordained, that we must learn from the Middle Kingdom navigation, metallurgy and above all the characters that embody sound. But Tlacaelel saw writing as primarily a tool of statecraft, religion, culture. It was my cousin Nezahual-coyotl, king of Texcoco, who became the true architect of Anahuac poetry, discovering, as had your own forefathers, that written verse has power."

There was a collective gasp as she lifted her brush and dipped it into the bowl of ink. With quick, supple moves of her wrist that belied her years, Macuilxochitzin flowed lovely characters down the page. An understudy stepped to the platform as she finished, and with a flourish he removed the paperweight and held the poem up for all to see.

The ink quivered upon the paper, glistening and vibrant. Alive. Many whispered the words to each other, partaking in the spread of creative energy.

"Bright Feathered God, / with blossoms you paint us to life— / divine calligraphy."

Bowing her head slightly, the poet acknowledged the heightened awareness her work had caused. "Inspired by one of my cousin's most famous poems. The lesson is simple. The Creator has drafted us into existence, his ink that holy substance that underlies the universe: teotl or ki. We manipulate that same teotl with our brushes. It trembles along our limbs, arising from the act of creation, and if we use the right ink, it imbues the characters with divine energy. The gods feed on it as they would a sacrifice, sated by the outpouring of our souls. They are pleased.

"The implications are clear. We believe in the ascendency of Anahuac. We trust that our destiny is manifest in the success of our endeavors. Patriotic verse written in calligraphy cements our nation's hegemony, and so the proper subject of serious poets is eulogy, the immortalizing of the great, the praise of warriors slain in battle, the eternal renewing of the Empire's strength. Our example should be Hitomaro, whose devotion to the Empress Jito centuries ago is still unparalleled. Of her, he famously wrote 'Even mountains and rivers / therefore together serve / our Sovereign as a goddess.' Let us strive for that same fealty today."

With a subtle gesture, Macuilxochitzin ceded the floor to Sogi, who gave a single vigorous clap and smiled.

"Well said, my Lady. Your own poetry and the works you cite thrill my heart, stir my love for our magnificent hybrid nation. As you point out, poets of our islands have for centuries known of this power. We uncovered the secret of dew from taro leaves, took the magic beyond what the Middle Kingdom had begun. And, indeed, it has long been our tradition to ensure that our culture endures and spreads.

"Yet, for those who practice Rinzai Zen, our reasons stem from the three marks of existence: its emptiness, its suffering, its impermanence. Life is made rich and poignant precisely because of how fleeting it is. When we accept that we are nothing, that we will suffer, that we will fade away, we discover beauty and meaning in our broken loneliness."

Sogi closed his eyes, calling up words. "Lord Nezahualcoyotl himself spoke of this hollow, painful intransience:

In vain was I born.
in vain I emerged
from the House of the Sun
to walk this bitter earth
and live a wretched life.

"Yet for all that, the philosopher king told us to rejoice, to sing and drink life to the deepest dregs:

Though the labor be in vain, my friends,
take pleasure in our song, our song.
Pick up your precious drums and beat!
Shake loose the flowers, spread them well—
even if they finally wilt!

Quiet laughter greeted this sentiment, and the priest rubbed a spotted hand across his shaven head. "In that respect he reminds me of Ikkyu, the irreverent monk and poet who delighted in shocking us into enlightenment. Once, a man near death who wanted Ikkyu to leave his bedside told him, 'I came alone and must go alone as well.' Laughing, the monk replied, 'Coming and going are delusions, friend. Look—I'll show you the path upon which nobody comes or goes.' Everyone talks of heaven, but perhaps we're already there, yes? Nezahualcoyotl told us 'It's not true / that we come to live on earth— / we only come to dream / then we rise from our slumber.' Ikkyu summed it up thus: 'You're the only koan that matters.' I love that. Look, my brothers and sisters."

Sogi twirled his brush mischievously, then spat into his bowl of ink before dipping it. Fluid motions like a dance, broken abruptly by a jester's flailing jerk, and his poem was complete. Gently he lifted it, turned it to his audience, recited the lines.

We may realize
that people are merely dreams—
the house abandoned,
its wild garden becomes home
to a swarm of butterflies.

As he said the last word, the characters rearranged themselves on the mulberry paper into inky moths that fluttered from edge to edge, delighting everyone gathered. Even Macuilxochitzin had to smile as the monk pantomimed shooing his animated words back into position.

"As you can see from my esteemed colleague's antics," she said, suppressing a laugh, "adding a bit of one's self markedly increases the power of the creation. But what the Nahua bards discovered under my cousin's tutelage was startling—magic like nothing we had imagined. Give a master poet amatl paper from the Nahua home-land, let her write upon it with Nipponese ink using characters from the Middle Kingdom, and behold!"

She laid a thick sheet of mottled brown paper on her writing table, turned away from the crowd to dribble spit into her ink, and then drew her brush quickly down the page.

"The Kyoto gardens / before the fireworks— / every heart feels peace."

An amazed, contented sigh rose collectively from those gathered. Sogi himself closed his eyes and grinned, tears dampening his cheeks.

The Mexica princess surged unexpectedly to her feet. "In the right hands, with the right tools, poetry can quite literally move the soul. But that is just the beginning, dear imperial subjects. My ancestors, too, had their secret sorceries. At the dawn of this age, when the newly formed sun struggled to leave the horizon, the Feathered God led all the other deities to bleed themselves in sacrifice, giving movement to that diurnal light. Blood, you see, is concentrated teotl."

From her skirt, she drew forth a long maguey thorn and pierced the index finger of her right hand. As blood welled, a darker red than anyone could credit, Macuilxochitzin smeared calligraphy down the inside of her left arm, raising it for all to see.

"A thousand orange blossoms / fall upon their heads."

Materializing from nowhere, mandarin flowers showered down on the crowd. The people, though they had heard of such deeds before, were struck dumb with astonishment, simply stretching out their hands to catch the white petals.

Sogi gathered blooms to his chest with a blissful expression, bent his head to take in their sweet perfume. Wordlessly, the monk stood and stepped down from the platform. Turning to face the shogun, who had been watching from the bridge, he gave a deep bow. Then he began to wander through the garden, searching. He came upon a cherry tree, its green leaves naked of blossoms this late in the summer. On the ground below it was a fallen branch, dried to a brittle brown.

"Look, my friends," he called, walking back toward the brook. "The fleeting world. Spring comes, flowers, drops to the soil. Summer begins the browning. Autumn brings the gold. Then comes winter, quiet death for all. Yet the greatest magic is imbedded in the world. Ikkyu knew this, and he cautioned those who seek knowledge elsewhere:

> Day after day priests pore over Dharma
> and endlessly chant their intricate sutras.
> Yet before all that nonsense, they should first
> learn to read the love letters sketched
> by wind and rain, by snow and moon.

The monk gestured at the water. "Oh, beloved, look on the wonders of this humble, broken world."

His hand moved so quickly that the characters he sketched upon the surface with that stick could be read before the slow current dragged them away.

"For a moment / the river of heaven / flows among them."

Sogi drew away with a strange little hop, and the brook leapt from its course, twisting serpentine through the air, rushing toward the crowd, and weaving itself among them. Children shouted with delight and splashed each other, but the adults were overcome with awe as they looked upon gilded koi swimming through the air within that miraculous stream.

A minute later, the water had poured itself back within its banks, and the crowd burst into thunderous applause.

Macuilxochitzin descended, approached Sogi, bowed. With a weary shrug of his shoulders, he reached out and drew her to him. She did not resist his embrace.

The shogun returned to the platform, lifting his arms in a call for attention. "Beautiful and enlightening! Yes, we are short-lived. That is why our prayers, our poetry, have such worth, such power. Brother Sogi and Princess Machuilxochitzin have shared different facets of a single truth with you. Life is fleeting. Enjoy what you can. But contribute whatever magic you receive from the gods to the things that last longer, the things you love, the things that you would leave to others. Family. Culture. Empire. Now, go, residents of Kyoto. Night will soon be upon us, and there are still many more festivities to be cherished before Tanabata concludes!"

At his command, the crowd dispersed, taking with them stories that would live for generations. The poets tarried by the brook for a time and then retired in silence to their pavilions.

Gradually the skies darkened over the city, revealing the glittering stars and the true River of Heaven, milky and bright, low on the horizon.

People gradually made their way into the hills. Special teams of pyrotechnicians—trained by experts from the Middle Kingdom, where the art had been perfected—launched a spectacular show over the roofs of the city. Fireworks danced fleetingly in the sky, leaving smoky traceries that were wisped away by gentle breezes.

Those gathered near Shokoku-ji temple noticed the two elderly poets standing together, looking up at the display, leaning heads together, whispering. Any apparent tension between them had dissolved as the evening wore on.

After the fireworks, most throngs disbanded as folk went home for more intimate companionship and sleep after the draining, joyful day. But the most pious, penitent and poetic drifted to the temple steps, their amatl tanzaku strips in hand.

The full moon silvered the swaying bamboo as the head of the temple lit a bonfire in the courtyard. In small groups, people approached and tossed their poems on the flames, watching ash and charred bits of paper spiraling toward the heavens.

Finally Sogi and Macuilxochitzin approached with their own onegaikoto. Rather than drop them on those lambent tongues of flame, they dipped the amatl sheets into the fire and turned away, the poems alight in their hands.

Together, in an elegant, elaborate dance, they wrote upon the empty air with burning paper. Characters hung suspended like red-orange afterimages, retaining their shape for the space of several heartbeats.

> Flickers of flame
> we twist briefly on the wind
> yearning to be stars.
> Take us in your hands, O gods—
> create a galaxy.

Then, as the poets stood hand-in-hand at the heart of the temple, their poem dissolved into sparks that drifted up into the night, losing themselves in the River of Heaven that flows from Kyoto to Tenochtitlan and on into eternity.

QUINTESSENCE

T WAS THE DAWN OF THE VERY LAST DAY, AND YET DR. ANAYELI Morelos had no regrets.

She stepped from her depa complex in the heart of Puebla—Angelópolis to its residents—squinting at the harsh glare of the sun. Even this early on a Monday the sidewalks bustled with a mix of working-class poor and 'toothed avatars of the middle class, plus the occasional municipal afandroide, cleaning or patrolling with impassive diligence.

Ducking out of the way of a motorized food shack that pulled to the curb and tilted solar panels to optimal, Anayeli subvocalized and turned on her e-lenses. Instantly, a virtual interface flickered to life, layering itself over the real world. Pinned labels popped up over key features of the cityscape, certain buildings glowed to indicate strategic importance, and individuals of no calculable significance were gray-scaled and faded so she could focus on her biggest concern.

Am I being followed?

As she scanned the crowd for possible threats, she muttered a few commands and a window opened up before her, appearing to hover on the left. With a quick flick of her hand, she scrolled through messages, mail and feeds. Nothing had been tagged. For the moment, it seemed she was safe.

Nodding to herself, she gestured her GPS on, and her lenses laid a glowing strip of arrows across the cracked and uneven sidewalk. This was the only sort of alteration she allowed herself. Guidance. Others were not so disciplined. It was the vogue to transform the world. Bigots erased the color and ethnicity of their fellow citizens, homogenizing their surroundings. Progressives filtered out ugly truths of human nature. Extreme religious types imposed piety and excised sin. Whether using e-lenses in physical form or viewing the world through an avatar's robotic eyes, people preferred illusion.

The younger set went even further. Skinning, they called it. Their environment became a medieval landscape, a teeming hell, an interstellar paradise, an underwater demesne. Humans were draped with the forms of animals, demons, merfolk, naked demi-gods, inscrutable aliens.

Anything not to see.

And so the world fell further into decay. As climate change ravaged the environment and technology put pleasures within arm's reach, lives were lived increasingly within a few dozen square meters. Architecture had simplified, become functional. Now, in the latter half of 2065, afandroides maintained the major metropoleis, but small towns atrophied, as had Anayeli's native San Juan Bautista Lo de Soto in Oaxaca State.

Ten billion people, deliberately blind.

Not Anayeli. Oh, she had once refused to see, but then everything she loved had been taken from her. Now it was her duty to see. Not just the visible symptoms of the moral sickness that ravaged the globe, but the underlying spiritual afflictions as well.

Steeling herself, she sprinkled ash into the palm of her hand from a small phial. Then she spat on it, using her fingers to mix up a blot of muddy paste which she smeared at the center of her forehead.

Here it goes.

Taking a deep breath, she enunciated the Nahuatl spell. "Ma itto moch."

Let all be seen.

Twining lines of fiery force shimmered into existence all around her, revealing a reality that undergird the world much like the world itself underlay her virtual interface. It streamed down in waves from the sun, webbed between the few plants along the streets, ebbed from patches of soil and the brains of passing folk.

But much of the city was dark, devoid of the essential glow. Avatars and droids were free of its glittering intaglio. Entire blocks yawned blackly, bereft of the substance.

Quintessence.

It was a form of the dark energy Anayeli had been researching most of her adult life. The Aztecs had called it teotl. God-stuff.

The new layer of data was essential to her mission. Immediately she noticed patterns of quintessence around certain pedestrians—there went a shapeshifter, her animal soul writhing eagerly in golden spirals; along came a sorcerer, hands and mouth smeared with god-stuff.

Then there were the ghosts, tethered to tragic places where they shambled and shook or gliding aloft on currents of teotl.

And slumbering beneath her or looming in the mountainous distance were the gods: vast and quiescent, their non-baryonic bulks glowing like suns.

Keeping her eyes focused on the earth itself, Anayeli made her way toward the neighborhood garage, on the lookout for the emergence of those complex spiritual patterns that her rivals generated. It was highly unlikely that her mission had been discovered by agents of the present obsolete and decrepit order, but she was sworn to a fanatical vigilance. The future of the cosmos depended on her actions today.

No human or supernatural interference. Time to move.

Taking the dusty, long-abandoned stairwell, Anayeli climbed to level six. Her vehicle hummed to life at her approach.

"Omega Lambda Center," she subvocalized as the hatch hissed open. She ducked inside, ensconced herself in the couch, and dialed the top hemisphere transparent so she could keep an eye out for possible threats. "Use the Tube."

The little ovaloid vehicle wheeled its silent way out of the garage and along the streets of Puebla till it came to the nearest Tube tower. It then slipped into the next available pod and was hoisted to the Tube. The vacuum initiated, and the scientist was soon speeding down the maglev rail toward her destiny.

The first time Anayeli saw the Dance of the Devils, she was just four years old. Her grandmother held her hand as they walked to the center of town on All Souls' Day. The music started, syncopated drums and whistling flutes, and twenty dancers shuffled into the plaza, taking widespread and stomping steps, bent at the waist, arms swaying rhythmically. They wore boots and furred leggings, capes of many colors that swirled when the dancers spun.

Young Anayeli gasped at their faces, not understanding that these were masks. Red and leering, horns twisting and spiraling from their heads.

In loud, terrifying unison, the dancers roared a single word: "RUHA!"

The girl drew breath to scream.

"Don't be afraid," her grandmother whispered in her ear, kneeling beside her. "Tata Terrón is coming, and so is Nana Minga. They'll guide the spirits. Nothing bad will happen."

A demoness threaded her way seductively through the troupe, an infant clutched to her breast. Though she tried to distract the dancing devils, an older figure came rushing toward her, wielding a whip as he gyrated. Between them, Minga and Terrón managed, seducing and scourging, to herd the troupe toward the cemetery, where Anayeli lost sight of them at last.

It wasn't until she was much older that her grandmother, a renowned folklorist, began to explain.

"Our ancestors were brought to Mexico from Africa. All parts of it. While this country was still a colony of the Spanish crown, we worked fields and ranches. Some revolted, fled here to the Costa Chica. They encountered Zapotec tribes, found common ground with them. In time, slavery was overturned. Our grandmothers and grandfathers forged a new identity: Afro-Mexican, steeped in the indigenous and African cultures."

"So the dance is from Africa?" Anayeli asked.

"In a way. The Catholic priests wouldn't let us worship our native gods, and when we were slaves we weren't seen as human enough to worship the saints. So we dressed our gods up like demons and danced for them instead. Now they help us stay strong, resist evil. They guide the souls of our loved ones back to their resting place during the second Day of the Dead. They remind us of our debt to our ancestors."

Pushing aside her loose, dark curls, Anayeli squinted thoughtfully. "And what is Ruha? Why do they yell that name?"

"He's the fierce Lord of the Desert, my child. Before being enslaved in West Africa and shipped to the Caribbean, our grandmothers and grandfathers had already begun to hide the names of their gods due to the spread of Islam. So the name of the jealous and wrathful Creator, chief among gods, was obscured. Al-Ruha simply means 'the spirit.' The dancers clamor to him for freedom. Freedom from slavery. Freedom from the crumbling rule of civilized order. Freedom from the injustice that has twisted our world."

A sense of hope and dread fluttered in Anayeli's stomach at the thought. "Does he hear them, Grandmother?"

The older woman smiled wistfully. "Yes, dear. Yes, he does."

The ten-minute Tube trip took Anayeli over swathes of denuded land, spiritually benighted, teotl drained as technology, pollution, botanic homogeneity, and robotic strip mining reshaped the terrain into something unnatural.

Even a decade of seeing could not numb her to the violence humanity had done to the world. Tears flowed. She refused to look away. Orizaba loomed massive and pristine, glowing hale though climate change had stripped it of its cap of snow. Beside it stooped Sierra Negra, its slopes and summit glistening with steel and concrete, home to the most ambitious projects conceived by the National Institute of Astrophysics.

It was a vast dead sinkhole in the metaphysical fabric of Mexico.

Soon Anayeli slowed to a stop, her vehicle eased down onto the sensor-crammed blacktop. Unprompted, the onboard navigation daemon drove through automated checkpoints and along access tunnels to a massive lift on the mountain's western face that shot the scientist up toward her workplace.

The gleaming halls of the Omega Lambda Center were simultaneously familiar and menacing as Anayeli greeted receptionists and coworkers, bending face to biometric locks as she traveled deeper into the complex.

Susana Rivera, the systems engineer on Anayeli's team, stood as she entered their spacious circular office. A look of confusion with a hint of annoyance flushed the younger woman's light skin.

"Dr. Morelos! I thought you weren't coming in, either. Ignacio and Dr. Palomo kind of gave me that impression."

"Sorry, Susana. I know you wanted to clean up code before the next deployment. I just had a bit of a brainstorm. You know the drill. But, hey, you keep working on whatever you're doing. I've got simulations to run. Could just be a dead end. I'll tell you if we ought to actually try out my idea."

"Alright. Let me know."

The two worked all morning in separate cocoons of sounds and images, their e-lenses 'toothed into the government servers via highly encrypted short-range connections. Taking great care not to alert the systems sentinels, she began cobbling together in her virtual workshop all the disparate elements she'd developed over the past year or so. Once she had assembled the routines, she would shunt them into place and move as quickly as possible.

The Milky Way came over the horizon just after sunset.

Anayeli would be ready.

Karima Morelos had been a botanist; her husband Francisco, an energy engineer. They were collaborating on an alternate energy project in the waning years of the petroleum age when a strange industrial accident claimed both their lives, leaving their ten-year-old daughter in the care of her grandmother, Nicolasa. Children are resilient, and Afro-Mexican communities tightly knit, so with the help of family and friends, the girl managed her grief well, healing quickly and moving forward.

However, when she got dizzy with love during her high school years, neglecting her studies and ditching class, Anayeli was confronted by her grandmother with a brutal truth.

"Your parents' death was no accident, child. Men with deadly resources at their disposal were determined to keep ripping open the earth, sucking the marrow from her bones though they damned themselves in the process. And those men had my son killed, my son and your brilliant mother. Don't dishonor them. Take up the burden they laid down in death. Find the hidden energies that make the heavens spin."

The revelation transformed Anayeli. She broke up with her girlfriend and poured herself into school. Her grandmother encouraged her interest in physics and astronomy, using her academic credentials to get the teen unusual access to resources and experts. Anayeli blossomed. Aced her college entrance exams. Was accepted into the Instituto Politécnico Nacional. Graduated summa cum laude. Immediately began her doctorate.

It was during those postgraduate years that she met Itzayana Tuz, a brilliant woman from Yucatan whose profound understanding of physics was matched by the sensual beauty of her black eyes and hair, her soft chocolate skin. Their shared research grew into friendship, edged into passion, deepened into love. Their dissertations intertwined as did their souls.

At their joint graduation party, they announced their engagement to family and friends. All were delighted, except for Nicolasa Morelos, who offered a superficial smile but clearly had concerns.

"Grandmother," Anayeli muttered, cornering the folklorist. "Can't you at least be happy for me? You may not approve of my lifestyle or my wife, but I'd hoped you would want me to find joy and fulfillment."

"Not approve? Nonsense. Forgive me if I've made you feel that way, dear. The reluctance you sense in me has nothing to do with your marriage. I can't explain what unnerves me—I simply intuit a wrongness, like something's waiting in secret to attack you. Please, ignore me for the time being. I'm a silly old woman. Let me give you a kiss, and we'll forget my foolishness."

The ceremony was simple but beautiful, a score of folks on a beach of the Costa Chica, white linen and plumeria blossoms, vows in Mayan and Spanish, benediction sung to the goddesses of yore. Among the many gifts was an oddity—a gorgeous pre-Colombian urn in which some of the ashes of Anayeli's parents had been sifted together.

"It's morbid and gross," Itzayana complained during their honeymoon in Huatulco, "like your grandmother wants to ruin things for us. She obviously doesn't like me, for whatever reason, and now she gives us a memory of death on our wedding day. Please, I know you can't return it, but I don't want to see it. If you love me, you'll keep it out of our home."

Though having a reminder of her beloved parents would have been comforting, Anayeli agreed with little hesitation, placing the valuable gift in a safety deposit box.

Soon the newlyweds were both teaching at the Astronomy Institute of UNAM and living in a high-tech depa in Mexico City. Their co-authored articles disproving lambdavacuum solutions garnered them global acclaim, and they found themselves presenting at conferences around the world.

Anayeli saw little of her grandmother during those first seven years of her marriage. Even setting the matter of the ashes aside, Itzayana hadn't responded well to the coldness from the older Dr. Morelos, and Anayeli had gradually distanced herself from her remaining family to keep her wife content.

During Easter Week of 2052, Itzayana learned one of her dearest aunts had fallen seriously ill, so she took a flight to Mérida, insisting that Anayeli remain behind to wrap up work on an important grant proposal. Mere hours after her wife's departure, Anayeli received an unexpected dinner invitation from renowned physicist Eva Andrade, with whom she had taken several courses as an undergraduate and doctoral student. Honored and confused, she took an autonotaxi to the professor's home in the upscale suburb of El Pedregal.

An obsequious criandroide ushered her into a sort of parlor, where she found not only Dr. Andrade but also her grandmother, white hair cropped close to her mahogany scalp, looking older and wearier than ever.

"What is this?" Anayeli demanded.

"Ana, I'm not trying to ambush you," Nicolasa began.

"No? Then what the hell are you trying to do? And you, Dr. Andrade? What would possess you to get mixed up in our family issues?"

Andrade motioned with a pale, age-spotted hand. "Sit down, Anayeli. This is more important than personal squabbles. There are things you must know, now, before it is too late."

Taken aback by the ominous tone, Anayeli slumped into a chair, locking her gaze with Andrade's sea-green eyes. "Alright. I'm listening."

The physics professor folded her hands together on her lap. "Your grandmother and I belong to a ... group, you might say. A very ancient society of learned folk seeking to right the imbalances of this world. Armed with science and age-old lore, we have attempted for centuries to preserve the inherent wildness of the cosmos, the unruly beauty that abides where man's crippling order has not siphoned necessary chaos away.

"Sadly, we have been unsuccessful. Evolving, ubiquitous technology has uprooted diversity, spread sameness to every nation, leveled our lives to patterned mediocrity.

"So the time for drastic measures has come at last. That is what we must discuss."

Anayeli shook her head, turned to her grandmother. "Drastic? What exactly does that mean?"

Nicolasa Morales sighed. "Do you remember Ruha?"

Andrade sighed. "Nico, wait. We have to ease into that."

Narrowing her eyes, Anayeli leaned forward. "What, the desert god? From the dance?"

Her grandmother nodded, ignoring Andrade's warning. "Yes. You see, he is an avatar of chaos. The Aztecs called him Tezcatlipoca. Your wife's people named him Juraqan, Raging Hurricane, nature unfettered. He has had enough. He wants to crack open the heavens and remake the world. And you, my dearest one, have been chosen to work his will."

For the space of several moments, Anayeli couldn't find any words. Then she clenched her fists and stood. "Are you two out of your fucking minds? What sort of strange hallucinogen have you been ingesting to come up with this shit? I mean, I know my grandmother indulges in that sort of thing, like a lot of the wackos in the soft sciences do. But you, Dr. Andrade? Shame on you."

She turned to leave.

"It's your wife," Eva Andrade called after her. "You must be careful of your wife."

She drew up short, spun around to face them. "Shut up. Don't you dare talk about Itzayana."

"She's not who you think she is," Nicolasa interjected. "My intuition was right. She's an agent of the other side, those who would pave the world, replacing nature with artifice. They know who I am, whom I serve. They've been tracking you since your parents' death, and they got you to fall for one of them, someone who can keep an eye on you, prevent you from your mission."

Anayeli felt nauseous bile rise, burn the back of her throat. "You joyless fucking hag. You never wanted me to have someone else to love. After Mom and Dad died, you wanted me for yourself, and it tears you up inside that I can live and thrive without you. Well, we're done, do you hear me? Don't ever contact me again."

"Listen," Dr. Andrade insisted, getting to her feet with a wobble. "Feel whatever indignation you must. But look to your wife. When the time comes that you suspect, take a pinch of your parents' ashes, mix it with saliva from your own mouth, and smear it on your forehead. Then repeat the word 'see' until you are able to. There's a spell that works faster." Here she spoke three words in Nahuatl.

Anayeli said nothing in reply to this almost sacrilegious suggestion. She simply left the residence with a lurching stomach and racing heart.

A week later, Itzayana returned. Her aunt's health had improved, she said. Life resumed its normal routine, though a part of Anayeli subtly analyzed her wife's behavior for traces of betrayal. There was, of course, nothing to detect. In fact, their conversations began to turn toward the idea of broadening their family, of motherhood.

Then the job offer came from the National Institute of Astrophysics—a chance to get in on the ground floor of the new Omega Lambda Center.

Itzayana responded with feigned indifference, clearly jealous of her wife's career opportunity.

"I suppose you should take it, but there are a lot of students who'll miss out on your great teaching and guidance. And you'll just be a very junior member of one of many teams. Hard to shine when you're surrounded by stars of that magnitude."

Anayeli drew the shorter woman into her arms, kissed the top of her head, rubbing palms against the tense muscles of her back.

"Oh, babe, don't worry. I'm sure that after I've been there a while, I can vouch for you. You know government officials. A judiciously given bottle of expensive tequila here, a serenade by mariachis there…"

Itzayana pushed her away. "I don't want your goddamn sympathy or help. I'm a better scientist than you, and I'll get where I'm going just fine on my own merits, thank you very much."

"Whoa. You're pretty pissed off."

"We had plans, Ana. What about taking a couple of years off, having a baby? You get this offer and suddenly it's all about you and not us, huh? That sucks, love. Really sucks."

Despite the arguments and misgivings, Anayeli ultimately accepted the position even given the considerable commute. Construction on Tube towers had begun, and she knew that soon this inconvenience would be resolved.

A few months into her work at the center, she began to notice something strange—a shaggy dog of indeterminate race, glimpsed out of the corner of her eye, always at the periphery of her vision. At first the animal seemed a stray that lived off refuse near Sierra Negra, but then she happened to see it on the streets of Mexico City, too, in clear defiance of the Animal Control droids.

Impossible. Can't be the same dog.

But she kept noticing it, though the black hound seemed to deliberately avoid her. She managed to capture images of it with her personal data device. It belonged to no breed on record. Its size was impressive, nearly that of a small human.

One day, on a whim, she called Itzayana from work, shortly after spotting the canine. There was no answer. Punching up the

Astronomy Institute, she learned that her wife had cancelled classes for the day because she was sick.

Inventing her own sudden illness, Anayeli returned to their apartment. Itzayana wasn't there.

When she did finally arrive, the couple had the ugliest fight of their eight years of marriage. Anayeli accused her wife of sleeping around and all sorts of other vices. Itzayana offered feeble excuses about working on a secret project for a private sector firm, but she refused to give any evidence.

Anayeli stayed the night in a hotel, heartbroken. She slept uneasily. Her dreams were full of darkness from which she was watched by a massive hound with her wife's eyes.

When she awakened, a strange impulse overcame her. She made her way to the bank, unlocked the safety deposit box, took a large pinch of ash in her hand.

An hour later, standing before the door of their depa, she spat into her hand, rubbed the paste on her forehead. "See," she muttered angrily. "See. SEE. SEE."

A blaze of fire seemed to wash across the world. She palmed the door open with a slap. Her wife stood in the kitchen, holding a spatula, and talking to someone through her earpiece.

"Call you back," Itzayana muttered. She lifted her eyes from the frying pan to look at Anayeli. "So, are we going to talk this thing out?"

But Anayeli couldn't reply. There, writhing golden and eager in the center of her wife's being, was that beastly dog.

Susana jerked her head up, startled and befuddled, trying to unfocus from the virtual world that blinded her to her physical surroundings.

"Sorry, Dr. Morelos! Kind of freaked me out there."

"No, problem. I should have pinged you first, given you a heads-up. Look, I've got an idea I want to try out. I could use your help in the Bubble."

Making small gestures that minimized her workspace, the tech nodded. "Of course. Let me just wrap something up real quick. Meet you at the lift."

They were soon traveling up through the heart of Sierra Negra. Anayeli thought of the supercollider spiraling around them, of the millions of muons trapped, decaying, of the trillions more that would be generated as she initiated the end.

Joy was not what she felt. No, the emotion was more akin to satisfaction or vengeance. Grim. Righteous.

The lift stopped at the Bubble, a domed work area at the summit containing the computer systems for multiple massive instruments, including the aging Large Millimeter Telescope and the Neutrino Beam Array. Anayeli unlocked the control bay for the latter, and the two women ducked inside its familiar contours.

The door cycled closed and locked behind them.

"Okay, boss. What's the plan?"

"I've got a new routine I want to upload that should optimize muon collection. Here, let's both log onto the system, then you can help me shunt the code over."

Two team members were needed for such an operation. It was the only reason Susana was there. That, and to keep her from interfering remotely. The woman was formidable when it came to systems.

The control console processed their biometrics, granted them access.

"Perfect," Anayeli said from behind Susana, dusting her palm with her parents' ashes, letting spittle dribble silently, her DNA blending with theirs, her teotl triggered by the traces of fiery death. "You'll find my code waiting in the queue."

Susana drew a sharp breath as she glanced at the subroutines. "Holy shit, Doc! You can't…"

Anayeli slapped her hand against the younger woman's forehead.

"Macamo ximolini," she rasped.

Susana went rigid, immobilized by sorcery, the quintessence in her flesh freezing her where she sat.

"Yes, I can," Anayeli whispered in her ear. "I'm the only one who can."

"What the fuck are you?" Anayeli shouted at her wife, raising a trembling hand to point at her. "What the fuck is that thing doing inside you?"

Itzayana clicked the stove off, tossed the spatula into the sink. "Goddamnit, Ana. You had to go and listen to them, didn't you?"

She took a step away from the kitchen, toward Anayeli, who eased out into the hall and held her hand above the palm plate, ready to slam the door shut and run like hell.

"Stay away from me, Itza. Or whatever your name is. Answer the question. What. Are. You."

Her wife lifted her hands, stopped where she was. "Okay, okay. Calm down. I'm a way pek, a shapeshifter. What you see is my animal self. A dog."

An ache pierced Anayeli's head and heart. She wanted to disbelieve, but the evidence was right in front of her. "You...you spied on me? You turned into a dog and followed me?"

"I had to, baby. Your grandmother—she's a fanatic. Wants to bring about the end of the world. We've been fighting her kind for centuries, Ana."

"We?"

"Agents of Light. Order. Children of the Feathered Serpent."

Almost doubling over with the nausea that flooded her, Anayeli groaned. "A lie? Us? It was just a lie? They sent you to keep an eye on me?"

Itzayana's face softened, her eyes reddened with tears. "Oh, sweetie, I know the way it looks. At first, yes, I was your watcher. But I fell in love with you. I ..."

"No! Shut up!" Anayeli gripped the door jamb, her vision coruscating with strange energies and grief. "All these years, all this time—and you're the enemy!"

"You don't understand!" her wife pleaded. "This dark god Nicolasa worships, Ruha or whatever she wants to call him, he is evil and so are his daughters. Bleak, fallen angels. Sealed away for eternity in a prison beyond the sky, another dimension. But there's a crack in the heavens, Ana, and your grandmother wants you to tear it open."

Anayeli drew a ragged breath. "So?"

"So? Don't you get it? Everyone will die!"

Heart thundering with betrayal and broken rage, Anayeli managed to whisper.

"Maybe that's what they deserve. Raped the world. Killed my parents. Ripped away my love. To hell with them and their goddamn machines."

The hound at the heart of Itzayana seemed to surge in a paroxysm of fury, and the woman's flesh burst asunder as it clawed its way out, howling and gnashing its teeth.

Anayeli cycled shut the door and ran.

Ran and ran and ran.

A decade later, her running was at an end. Every attempt at stopping her had been thwarted. Itzayana was long dead, along with every trace of compassion Anayeli had felt for all those blind human beings with their parasitic tech. They had had betrayed their sacred stewardship. If this stunted, tamed and toothless world was to be renewed, made savage and green and whole again, chaos must run wild.

The wheels of the cosmos forever turned. Life. Death. Rebirth.

It was time to complete the cycle once more.

She executed the subroutine. The supercollider hummed to life beneath her feet, accelerating particles at an unprecedented rate through its 40 kilometers of spirals. Smearing the last spit-moistened handful of her parents' ashes across the console, Anayeli muttered her final incantation.

"Ma tlapohui in teilpilcalli."

Let the prison be opened.

As the Milky Way came over the horizon, she adjusted the Horn, aiming it for the black cleft in that profusion of light. Seen with sorcery, the scar glowered with sputters of teotl, sign of the unspeakable forces that had struggled down the vast ages to get free.

With an audible roar, the neutrino beam burst from the summit of Sierra Negra, pouring into that rift at a spiritual level, buttressed by black magic and Anayeli's despair.

The cataclysmic clash created a loop, replenishing the muons and pions dying at the mountain's heart, feeding the beam.

The crack widened.

Without a glance at Susana, Anayeli left the control bay, palmed open the emergency exit. The shrill alarm meant nothing to her. Neither did the thin, keen winds that whipped around the mountaintop.

Turning her face to the heavens, Anayeli watched the cosmos rip open. Her limbs trembled in dread anticipation. She could not fathom what would come next, but it would be better than this nearly dead world.

Cyclopean talons thrust through the gap. She caught a glimpse of behemoth wings.

"Nana Minga!" she cried, overcome with horror and awe. "I'm ready to dance!"

SHRINE

MARISA EMERGED FROM THE LITTLE BRICK VAULT, blinking at the sun. Her back and knees ached from kneeling for nine hours at the makeshift prie-dieu. Her nose itched from the profusion of flowers. Her throat was worn raw from her hoarse prayers to Don Pedrito Jaramillo, the curandero who had died at this very spot a century ago after decades of healing the sick.

None of this discomfort overshadowed the migraine, throbbing sick and malevolent just beneath the skull on the right side of her head. It seemed to feed on the light and heat of the pitiless south Texas sun, unfocusing Marisa's eyes, sending the world spinning out of control until she doubled over and vomited up what little breakfast remained in her stomach.

"Are you okay, m'ija?"

Small, strong hands clasped her elbows, helped her to her feet. It was an older woman, perhaps fifty, a purple rebozo across her shoulders. Wearing a simple white blouse and embroidered skirt, she might have walked the streets of any border community during the last century and not been out of place. Letting Marisa lean on her, the woman guided her through a maze of tombstones to the shade of a nearby tree.

"Gracias, señora."

"It's nothing, dear. Migraines?"

Marisa nodded, rubbing her blurring eyes. "Yes. Bad."

"Ándale. I've seen cases like this before. Let me guess. Doctors prescribed drugs, but they just made the attacks a little less frequent.

So then you went to the hierberías and local curanderas, the sobadoras and shamans."

It hurt to speak or move with the pressure writhing within, so Marisa bent her forefinger in slight affirmation.

"Where are you from?"

"Mercedes," she managed to whisper. "In the Valley."

The older woman lifted her left foot, scratched between the straps of her huaraches. "Damn ants. Hmm. None of that worked, obviously. So you drove up here to Falfurrias, hoping that whatever essence Don Pedrito left behind might cure you, or that he might intercede for you there beyond. Bueno. Problem is, the kind of migraine you have? Needs much stronger magic, much older rituals."

Marisa hushed the woman gently. "Right now, just need … to sit in my car a bit. Help me?"

Together they stepped through the cemetery's creaking gate and crossed the uneven gravel of the turnout. Marisa eased behind the wheel of her car, wincing at the hot touch of the seat against her back. Starting the engine and turning up the AC, she gestured at the woman to get in as well.

"It's starting to fade," she explained. "Sit with me a while."

Beyond the hum of motor and fan, there was relative silence for the better part of a half hour. The migraine unclenched itself, leaving Marisa feeling slightly hung-over and depressed, with a soreness across her skull but no real pain.

"Thank you, ma'am," she finally said, giving the older woman's hand a brief squeeze. "Most people don't understand. They offer aspirin and advice and so forth, talking and talking, making it worse.

It's like they can't believe such a thing actually exists. My dad used to tell me I was making it up to get out of chores."

"Oh, I've been around all sorts of ailments, m'ija. Very familiar with migraines, though you've got a special case, I think. Tell you what. Why don't you let me buy you dinner? There's a little place close by on 281, Rick's, not much to look at from the outside, but they've got great food. You really need to eat after spending the day in that little shrine with such massive pain."

Marisa was starving, so she agreed, heading for Business 281 and letting the woman guide her for about a half mile to a greasy spoon beside a run-down gym. It was dim inside, and cool, which lessened the disorienting after-effects of the attack. *Postdrome*, the doctors called this stage. Marisa always thought of it as the slumber of some unspeakable parasite lodged in her brain.

"My name is Sara Manso," the older woman said after they had ordered cold Mexican cokes and tacos callejeros.

"Nice to meet you, Doña Sara. I'm Marisa Zabaleta."

"And what do you do there in Mercedes, Marisa?"

"I'm a paralegal." Worried that this sounded too haughty, she added, "At my Uncle Rosendo's firm."

"Boyfriend?"

Marisa pictured Bruno for a moment, features impassive as he told her he wanted to simplify his life. "Not anymore. I'm apparently too complicated. I have a dog, though."

"You're probably better off that way," Doña Sara mused.

"Yeah. Love's a little like the onset of a migraine. You get a weird euphoric feeling, start craving unusual foods, have mood swings. Your muscles tense up. Then the aura kicks in and you begin to see stuff. Your field of vision narrows, and you go all numb. Not totally unpleasant, just odd and a little inconvenient. But major pain is just around the corner."

"Yes, that sounds like my relationship with my first husband, rest his brutal soul."

A woman emerged from the kitchen, setting plastic plates and frosty bottles in front of them. As Marisa ate, she thought back over Doña Sara's words in the cemetery.

"You said I needed 'stronger magic' and 'older rituals.' What did you mean?"

The older woman leaned back, adjusted her rebozo. "Bueno, m'ija, I was born in Boquillas del Carmen, Coahuila, but my ancestors weren't Spanish. No, my people are the Chizo, and we have lived in the Big Bend area for centuries, taking on Mexican customs and language to fade away from the eyes of Westerners. In secret, though, many of us have continued along the Path of the Ancients."

Marisa tapped the surface of the metal table. "You're a shaman, aren't you?"

"Pos, sí. Can't deny it."

"And you were hanging out by the shrine to see if anyone needed 'healing,' huh?"

Doña Sara lifted a hand as if to ward off suspicions. "I know what you're thinking, but that's not the whole story. I have an older cousin who lives in Premont. She's been pretty sick for a while, and I came to help her husband with her treatments. But, yes, I do visit these sorts of shrines around the state. Sometimes I meet people who can't be helped by anyone else."

"Uh-huh." Marisa didn't want to doubt this woman, who so reminded her of her own mother and grandmother, but quacks and frauds had already taken so much of her money that she just had to be cautious. "Adelante. What's your pitch?"

The shaman's eyes sparkled, not with anger, but amusement. "There's a shrine in Big Bend National Park. A holy place for the Chizo near the mountains that bear our name. I've taken tough cases out there. I perform a complex ritual, and by its end I have rid them of their pain."

Marisa glanced at her knockoff purse in the chair next to her. "And how much would this cost?"

"Well, I've got to head back anyway, so if you save me the bus fare by driving me, I'll just charge you sixty dollars."

"Hang on." Marisa dug around for her cell phone and then used an app to calculate the distance. *Seven or eight hours. Two tanks of gas there, another two back. Add those eighty bucks to her fee …*

"I'm inclined to say yes, Doña Sara. At this point, I'm willing to try pretty much anything. But do you know of a really cheap hotel nearby? There's no way I'm driving all evening and into the night."

A smile crinkled the older woman's eyes. "Hell, if you don't mind sleeping near a vieja roncadora like me, I've got a room with two beds at the Oasis in Premont. We could hit the road at first light. ¿Cómo ves?"

It didn't take long to fall asleep. After calling her sister and asking her to watch Buddy for another couple of days while she sought treatment farther west, Marisa closed her eyes and slipped away from the waking world. Despite Doña Sara's warning about her snoring, she spent the night sunken into a deep, almost comatose slumber in which dark forms squirmed, but no sound or pain impinged.

The next morning they packed and ate a substantial breakfast of huevos divorciados, refried beans and diced potatoes, loading up on flour tortillas to tide them over till a planned late lunch in Del Rio. Stopping briefly at Wal-Mart to pick up some supplies, they headed east. The drive took them along aging two-lane highways, across the browning brushland, through sparsely populated towns.

Sara Manso was a spell-binding storyteller and attentive listener, like many of Marisa's own aunts, so it was easy to open up to her as the chaparral unfolded before them. They spent the first few hours swapping family stories, legends, recipes. Then the shaman spoke in general terms about her people, who once called themselves the Tacuitatome before others named them Chizos, a word that echoed with hints of forests, ghosts, arcane sounds.

Finally Doña Sara broached the subject of Marisa's condition.

"When did the migraines start? Puberty?"

"No. Doctors have told me that hormonal changes seem to trigger them in other women, which is why they're more severe when you're menstruating, but my first migraine came when I was seven. And they've been coming ever since, without any real rhyme or reason or predictability at all. Quién sabe. I think I'm a freak or something."

Doña Sara made a dismissive noise, but Marisa ploughed on.

"Seriously. For most of eighth grade, they disappeared. I thought going to CCD at church had cured me or something. But then came the day of my confirmation. When Bishop Peña touched my forehead with consecrated oil, a horrible burst of agony dropped me squirming to the ground. Apparently, I started screaming all sorts of obscenities, insulting the bishop, cursing the Church, threatening everyone who tried to touch me. I don't remember any of it. The pain was so overwhelming that I lost consciousness. When I woke up, my dad was pissed and my mom inconsolable.

"Well, that scene made it tough to go to mass for a while, as you can imagine. My parents thought I was possessed or something, but our priest consulted with my doctors and they ruled that out, thank God. But the migraines were back. I didn't get another one that bad till, well, till I had sex with Freddy Higuera in 10th grade, which I think traumatized him for life, pobrecito. But they were back. Occasionally at first, then more and more often. I had to switch to a charter school to graduate. Couldn't manage normal classes. Needed self-paced modules so that I could work around the inevitable attacks."

"And now?"

Marisa gripped the wheel more tightly. The road seemed to disappear on the horizon, to fade into the brambles and mesquite, as if quite soon the car would reach the edge of civilization and careen off into the unknown.

"Hardly a day goes by without one, Doña Sara. My uncle lets me work as I can, but it's just … impossible. I won't be able to make it much longer if I can't find relief."

The hollow desolation that had been emptying out her heart for years crept into her voice like a bleak echo in the midst of desolation.

"But if no one can help me—I guess there is always one way out, no?"

The shaman reached over and placed her palm over Marisa's clenched hands. "I swear to you again, m'ija: I will end this torment. The rites of my ancestors will set you free."

They had a quick lunch in Del Rio in the early afternoon, and then Marisa followed the calm yet insistent instructions of her GPS app till they arrived in Marathon around 4 pm. In the distance, mountains loomed blue and craggy, stooped titans struggling beneath the weight of the cloudless sky. Unnerved by their age-old silent stare, Marisa drove for another hour, heading south on 385 till she hit the park entrance at Panther Junction Visitor Center.

"Okay, m'ija. Turn right here on Ross Maxwell Scenic Drive. The trail we're looking for starts about eight miles down."

Before long, they pulled into a parking lot that overlooked a drop in the terrain. Below, Marisa could make out the ruins of a ranch house amid the tall grass and cactus. The native stone walls were still standing, though the glass had long ago been shattered and the wooden porch weathered down to the dull gray of driftwood.

"Blue Creek Canyon," Doña Sara explained. "All this used to be the Homer Wilson Ranch till the government acquired the land. Bueno, mira. About three hours of sunlight. That's enough. But you're gonna want to put some tennies on if you've got them. We have some hard walking ahead of us."

As Marisa changed her footwear and shouldered her backpack, the shaman slid a couple of bottles of water into a large, brightly colored woven bag she slung across her chest.

"Come on. This is the smoothest part, girl."

The trailhead was right at the edge of the pavement, and the two women descended along the road's short, moderate grade with little effort until they reached the flat bottom of the canyon. The declining sun slanted indifferently across other abandoned structures: a storeroom, the ruins of a bunkhouse, a weed-infested corral, rusted chicken coops. The land, free from the tenuous grip of men and horses, had begun to reclaim the wood and stone once gouged from its arid flesh. Flickers of unseen life disturbed the ochre brush, but beyond those small movements, the canyon was unnerving in its stillness.

Doña Sara pulled at Marisa's arm, and they continued along the trail, the pebbly gravel twisting awkwardly underfoot. Before them, denuded hills thrust stubbly chins at the sky. Strange ridges like stony brows and fairy chimneys that grasped the air in arthritic paroxysms added to the sense that cyclopean sentinels lay all about, buried beneath the sandy soil.

They headed north along a meager arroyo that sputtered over jagged rocks beside the dusty path. Marisa scanned the canyon wall closest to them. From time to time she noticed strange rust-red petroglyphs, primitive lines and spirals that hinted at shapes without ever finally resolving into an image. As she stared at one complex pattern, she felt a familiar fatigue settle, not normal exhaustion, but something more existentially draining.

"Another one's coming," she called to Doña Sara, who was setting a swift pace, even in her simple leather sandals. The shaman stopped, pulled a water bottle from her bag.

"Here, drink. How long till it hits?"

Marisa wiped her lips, screwed the cap back on. "An hour? I never know, really. Are we okay on time? I'd hate to hike back through this in the dark."

"Don't worry. It's only another two miles or so. But if we have to, if the ritual takes too long, we can camp up at Laguna Meadows. It'll be rougher than you're used to, pero ya. You can handle it."

The trail began a gradual climb. Odd cairns marked its increasingly indistinct margins. Soon they were walking between spindly hoodoos of copper-toned layered rock, strangely twisted pillars that reared like twining serpents three stories overhead. As the late afternoon light scintillated against their narrow length, the spires seemed to change color as if slowly uncoiling.

Averting her eyes in sudden fear, Marisa tried to blink away the blurry patch in her vision, hoping it was just a result of sun glare. But no. It was her body, betraying her as it always did, bleeding away her eyesight so that when the pain came it would find her floundering in a dim, grey limbo.

She could feel despair rising like a steady tide. All these years. How many friends have I lost because this thing pushes them away? How much of life have I missed out on? Her family and a few close girlfriends had stuck by her, but she could see in their shared glances that their love was frayed by the attacks. Everything crumbles before it. Even my faith is unraveling. The santeras and priests can sense it. They say that's why no one has been able to heal me. But what do they expect? How could God do this to me? Why? And if not Him, who? And if there's no one doing it, if it's just random shitty luck, then what's the point?

They reached the arroyo's source, a small bubbling spring that sustained a thicket of oaks. Marisa rested for a moment in that shade, splashing the cool water on her face and neck. Her field of vision was narrowing. As Doña Sara urged her on, the world shrank, encircled by darkness. Hemianopsia, the doctors called it. She stepped back onto the sunlit path. The air flickered around her, ambient light fritzing and jagging in black and white lines.

"Oh, God, Doña Sara," she cried out. "This is going to be one of the really bad ones."

"Keeping walking, girl. Not far now."

They continued climbing, heading toward the juniper-pinyon pine woodlands that encircled a blocky tor up ahead. Keeping her failing eyes on the shaman's back, Marisa forced her feet to move. A ringing started up in her right ear, low and persistent at first, then louder and louder till it became a dull roar. The landscape tilted. Marisa stumbled.

"Here." The shaman thrust a think branch in her hand. "Lean on it. I can't carry you, así que aguanta. A little ways yet."

There was no way. She couldn't do it. Every step was like dragging her entire body forward, using the walking stick as a lever. The sky whirled dim and empty above her.

A hand on her shoulder. "Rest a second, child."

The canyon rim was a battlement. Dark forms kept watch. Beasts. Men. Demons. Roiling silhouettes against the deepening blue. Beyond them, all around, the behemoths raised their crooked backs to the cosmos, streaked with layers of limestone, antediluvian scars that hinted at stony fangs and claws.

"Do you see it? Look." The woman seized her jaw firmly, turned her head. There, a gaping hole in the wall, a black maw yawning above a brambly escarpment. "The shrine."

Pain erupted in Marisa's skull, a continuous writhing stream of agony that unhinged her mind. Falling to her knees, she began to scream. Strong fingers forced something bitter into her mouth, squeezed water between her lips, roughly massaged her throat till she swallowed against her will.

The migraine did not subside. It raged against the prison of her brain. But Marisa no longer shuddered or moaned. Her body went numb, muscles refusing her broken commands. She tumbled into the weeds, unmoving.

Doña Sara grabbed her arms and began to drag her up the steep incline. Beneath the purple rebozo that shaded her face, the woman's eyes were devoid of sympathy, of mercy. Above, the sky was darkling.

Time lurched. Chalky cave walls smudged black from fires. Rust-red enigmatic petroglyphs. The shaman opened her bag, drew forth a small bow and a long shaft of bone ending in a hollow copper cylinder with jagged teeth.

Marisa tried to cry out, but her despair just gurgled weakly in a clenched throat.

"Calla, madre," Doña Sara muttered, her impassive features softening for a moment. "'Blessed are you among women.' Isn't that the phrase? It must emerge, querida. You're the gateway and the sustenance."

The woman turned Marisa's face away, set the bow drill against her temple, chanted obscure words in a forgotten tongue. The sun was setting behind the south rim. The sky bled red and purple into the growing black.

Ecstatic shouts. "Sinauhé! Sinauhé!"

A sharp bite. The whine of metal on bone. Relief that brought tears to her eyes.

The thing inside her uncoiled, slithered through the hole in her skull. As the light failed, it reared above her, unspeakable and ungodly, twisting and glistening black, before dropping to devour the husk of its unwitting mother.

THE TEEN
AND THE TRITON

As Linda loaded her tray with the rest of the dishes, her father walked over to snag the 50-dollar bill the large party had left as a tip.

"Need to borrow this, kid," he said to her astonished expression. "Pay you back soon, I promise."

Linda straightened and backed away from the tray, feeling nauseous and angry. "Really, Dad? It's been slow all day. You don't pay me to wait tables. All I get is tips, and you're going to start ripping me off, too?"

Pete Casas' sun-weathered face went cold. "Look, I owe some money. I'm going to take this, play some blackjack tonight, and tomorrow you'll have your pinche fifty bucks to blow on books or whatever goddamn thing you want."

"Unless you lose, which you normally do."

Her father growled low in frustration. "Wow, you're just like your mother. Siempre chingando la madre."

That's it, Linda thought. I'm out of here. She walked over to the register, grabbed the keys, and burst through the doors into the late afternoon rays of a golden June sun. Walking quickly along the marina boardwalk, she reached the slip where their flat-bottomed motorboat was moored to a salt-eaten pylon. Untying the line, she jumped down into the boat and slammed the key into the ignition.

"Linda!" her father shouted. He was standing at the entrance to the Southpoint Grill, the family restaurant. "Where are you going? How'm I supposed to get home?"

"Ask one of your gambling buddies to give you a ride!" she shouted. "Or call Grandma Chenta and explain why I left you here. I don't give a shit!"

Linda started the engine and guided the boat in an arc away from the marina, gradually heading north-east across the Laguna Madre, the bay that separated Port Isabel from South Padre Island. There was a good chop on the water, and as she opened the throttle for more speed, the boat began to slap against the waves like a bucking bronco. She tried not to think of her stupid life, her parents' divorce, her suck-ass junior year at Port Isabel High (after Robert had dumped her for a cheerleader), her lack of money or friends or plans for the future ...

She gazed out at the white-flecked green of the bay, sea-weed dancing just below the surface, a dark undercoat for the scintillating waves. Gulls called to one another. The smell of salt and sun filled her lungs. Such beauty distracted her for a while.

Then, as she passed under the two-mile-long Queen Isabella Causeway, marveling at the massive support columns that stretched eighty feet above her, a strange figure caught her eye: what appeared to be a body, floating near a huge concrete footing.

Throttling back, she looped around and pulled alongside the form, her heart racing. Did someone drown? Did a cartel dump some corpse into the bay?

She killed the engine and leaned over for a closer look. It appeared to be an attractive young man with long black hair. Bare-chested, the youth was mired from the stomach down in a clump of seaweed that anchored him in place. His skin was tinged with a strange greenish pallor.

Oh, fuck. He's dead.

With a shuddering sigh, Linda reached for the radio, meaning to call the harbormaster and report the body. Unexpectedly, though, the corpse opened its eyes. They were green, a startling green like sunlight filtered through ocean depths, and they fell on her pleadingly. Reaching out a hand, the young man gurgled incomprehensible syllables at her.

His hand was webbed like a frog's, the tissue between his fingers a translucent pink.

What the…?

He gurgled again, and she shook her head. "I can't understand you, but I'll get you help. Just hang on." She repeated herself in Spanish, just in case. His eyes widened.

"N-no," he managed to burble at her. "Na…da de ayu…da."

"Okay, Spanish then," she muttered, and then spoke in that language. "Are you in trouble with the law? Is that it?"

"In trouble. Yes. Help me."

Shaking her head at the insanity of it, Linda began to work. The waves had pushed the boat farther and farther away, so she first circled the footing slowly and then made a loop in the mooring line, tossing it to the youth. "Put it around your chest and I'll pull you out," she said.

He did as she told him, and she slowly opened the throttle, towing his body free of the morass. Hand over hand she drew him closer to the boat till she could reach over the side and grab hold of his slippery arms. She began hauling him onboard, and he clung to her desperately, his body shivering with either cold or pain.

With a final grunt of exertion, Linda yanked him completely into the boat, and stepped back as he flopped onto the deck.

"Holy Mother of God," she whispered.

From the waist down, the youth was a fish. A nasty bite of some sort oozed redly on the left side of his...tail.

"What are you?" she demanded with a start.

"Waykay. Tritón." His voice was a pained gasp.

A triton? Linda read voraciously. She loved mythology. She knew about that legendary race. She almost smiled at her dawning realization.

I just rescued a goddamn merman!

He tilted his head back, searching for her eyes. His pained, jade-green gaze bored into her.

"Help me," he whispered.

An hour later, Linda was rigging an old fishing net in the empty berth beside her father's at the condominium complex they called home. When she was done, the net was nearly completely in the water, its edges tied to the two pylons and docks on either side. The triton, who was clinging to the side of the boat (he had told her being completely out of the water was painful), placed his webbed hands on the nearest dock and edged around it to the neighboring slip, where he let go with a sigh, kept from floating away by Linda's jury-rigged system.

"Thank you," he muttered, submerged to his chin.

Linda lowered herself to the edge of the boardwalk and slipped her bare feet into the water. "No problem."

He closed his eyes and leaned back into the net, only his nose and mouth exposed to the evening air. "You have questions."

"Uh, yeah. I have questions. But you're hurt."

"Do not worry. Ask whatever you want."

"Well, what's your name?"

The triton hesitated, then sang a burbling series of tones that made Linda shiver.

"It means … *Light That Slants through Calm Seas.*"

She repeated the phrase to herself in English. "Can I just call you Light for short?"

"Light." He seemed to weigh the word on his pale lips. "Yes. I like the sound. What is your name?"

"Linda."

"Linda. *Kind. Pretty.* Yes. This is a good name. Very short but packed with meaning."

She had never really thought about the meaning of her name, but his strangely accented, lilting voice gave it an air of mystery. He thinks I'm kind. And pretty. She blushed a little in the darkling.

"How do you know Spanish?"

"My mother. She was human once, a teenager in Mexico. But siren blood was her family heritage, and when the call came from the depths, she responded. Ages ago, sirens left the sea, married men, had children who appeared human, created hybrid bloodlines down the years. As the centuries passed, our numbers dwindled. Then in recent times, our leaders discovered how to draw those cousins back to their ancestral homes. Our race has been strengthened, and we once again know about the human world."

Light shifted in the netting and winced.

"Your wound hurts, doesn't it?" Linda leaned forward, peering through the water at the bite. "Anything I can do to help?"

"No. The water of this bay is saltier than the sea, and we are a hardy race. All I need is time and rest."

"So what happened? It looks like a shark bite to me."

Light floated still for a time, his black hair a medusa coiling in slow sinuous waves. Without warning he dipped his face underwater. When he resurfaced moments later, his voice was wistful, more refined.

"My mother Renata wed a king, ruler of a bright realm: vast, interconnected caverns lit by magma streams and bioluminescent algae. It is known as ..." Here he crooned lilting syllables in bubbling currents of sound. "Glowing Grottoes Strung Like Pearls. Many daughters were born to them, and finally I entered the bosom of the sea, their hoped-for prince. Long had my father sought to ally with the other kingdom that lies on the easternmost edge of what you call the Gulf of Mexico. Yet their ruler had but a daughter, so my sisters had been of no use in this negotiation."

Linda nodded slowly. "They married you off."

He shook his head. "I was merely betrothed. The union is to occur at the next full moon."

"I don't understand. What are you doing in the bay, then?"

"I have escaped. I have no desire to wed some siren whose face I have never looked upon. How can I give her my heart? Would you do so, agree to spend your life with a man you do not know?"

"Uh, no. Well, probably not. It's just, hrm, if he were a prince... Dude, that would be hard to say no to, especially if my family needed me to make the sacrifice and he wasn't ugly or an idiot or something ... But, yeah, no. That's lame."

"Precisely. I fled west, aided by loyal dolphins. We were attacked by a wayxoc, however. A sentient shark."

Loyal dolphins? Sentient sharks? It all seemed ridiculous, but Linda was sitting there talking to a merman, so she kept her mouth shut.

Who knows what other crazy crap is actually real? This changes everything.

"I was pursued into these shallow waters before my assailant turned away. Thus you discovered me, exhausted and at my wits' end."

"Wow. This is pretty overwhelming. Okay." She stretched until her bones popped. "Rest. I can help you with that. No one uses this slip, and the owners of the next one over won't be back for weeks. You may have to slide down deeper when my dad comes around, but other than that, you're cool. What about food, though? What do you eat?"

Light opened his sea green eyes and gave a slight smile. "Fish, as you might imagine. Some species of seaweed. Turtle eggs. Never the flesh of a mammal."

Linda thought about the conditions under the sea. "And none of this would be cooked, huh."

"Not often, no, though in our kingdom we occasionally sear shrimp in magma-heated devices."

Yanking her feet from the water, Linda stood and then nodded decisively.

"Okay, then. Fish I can handle. Dad may screw most other things up, but he taught me how to bait a hook and reel the big ones in."

That evening, while her father was off gambling with her tips, they established a ritual. Linda would sit on the dock, casting her line and waiting for a bite. As the moonlight glittered silver on the dark green of the bay, she would tell Light of her depressing life: her mother's affair, the ugly divorce, the months spent living with her mother and grandparents in Camargo, her decision to move back with her father. Light listened attentively as she explained how her father's mom set up the restaurant to keep him out of trouble, never expecting him to cook the books and siphon off profits for his gambling habits.

Light in turn talked about the kingdom of Glowing Grottoes, its beauties and defects, its virtues and vices. Much like humans, sirens and tritons loved, hated, helped, and betrayed one another. They were capable of incredible feats of skill and possessed deep, ancient knowledge, but they were nonetheless insanely prideful people prone to wage war for the most meaningless slight.

Each morning she rode with her dad to the marina, attended the lunch and dinner crowds, helped clean up. She smiled and was agreeable, even when he took her tips. They would ride back each evening, saying little but never fighting. Light would hide himself as the boat approached, and her father was never the wiser. When he would grab the car keys and mutter some excuse, Linda didn't bother to argue. She knew he was headed out to gamble their livelihood away, but Light needed her.

And every night for two weeks the ritual was the same. She caught fish. He ate them. They spoke late into the night. It was idyllic, and Linda found herself actually happy for the first time in months.

Eventually his wound had healed enough that Light began to swim a little, gradually building up the strength of his tail. On her day off, Linda joined him, donning her coral-pink bikini and braving the briny currents near the condo. She marveled at his grace in the water, how he sliced through the sun-dappled green, dipping and twisting, leaping from wave to another with a speed that took her breath away.

He's beautiful, she thought, and her throat tightened. She knew this emotion. It had snuck up on her before, with Robert. *What am I doing? I can't fall in love with a triton! That's fucking nuts.* But there it was, nonetheless. She couldn't deny what she felt.

As she swam toward his bobbing form, she noticed that he was observing her closely.

"It is unfortunate that your fingers lack webbing," he said as she neared him. "But if you were to cup your hands differently, thus—" He took her fingers in his, molded them to a particular shape. "There. That will lessen the drag."

Not wanting him to let go, Linda stuttered, "Uh, wh-what about the way you, uh, wriggle yourself through the water without using your arms? Can you—can you show me how to do that?"

Light smiled at her. "Certainly, Linda. Come, stretch out. Float still for a moment."

She did as he asked, the rocking of the waves moving her closer to him.

"Now, then, pull your arms close to your body. I will guide your movements."

He placed one hand on her legs, the other on her stomach. She almost shivered at his touch.

Oh, Linda, you're in big trouble, girl.

He guided her movements, showing her how to flex her waist and legs like a dolphin might. She was too giddy to do a very good job on her own.

As the sun began to set, they headed back to the slip; toweling dry, she went inside to make herself a sandwich. When she came back out, she found him delicately picking flesh from the bones of a sea trout.

"I was able to catch it myself," he explained. "Your nursing has worked wonders, Linda. Thank you."

She sat beside him, dangling her legs into the water. "Well, I should thank you. You've made my summer...made my life more interesting, just by showing up. I don't know how I'm going to be able to go back to school next month and act like there isn't a whole world of magical beings and shit beyond the boring life of a human girl."

"As I will find it difficult to forget such kindness and beauty. I should not ever want to forget. The world is a better place with you in it, Linda Casas."

"Yeah, well, at least one person thinks so."

"Come now. You have mentioned friends and family. Surely there are others who care for you."

"Sure, but...you know, not..." she trailed off, embarrassed.

"Not young human men, you mean to say." Light smiled mischievously. "Do you not have suitors, Linda, boys your age who seek your company?"

Robert's face flashed through her mind. She had managed not to think of him for two whole weeks. "I was dating this one guy for about six months, but he cheated on me with a cheerleader, and when I found out, he ditched me in front of my friends. It was pretty humiliating."

The triton's face darkened. "I see. Not a particularly noble character, this boy."

"No. Not really. I've got kind of shitty luck with human males, Light. Robert with his stupid cheerleader, my dad and his gambling—You know they want him to run for mayor of South Padre Island? Hell, if they knew what a loser he can be, they'd take that offer back in a hurry."

"But you love him."

Linda leaned back. Gulls swept back and forth overhead, smelling the remains of her sandwich and Light's fish. "Of course I love him. But what am I supposed to do? I can't be his parent. He's my dad! The roles are usually the other way around. I mean, to get him straightened out would mean—gah. I'd have to sacrifice a lot. And he wouldn't like it. It'd be an up-hill battle."

They sat in silence for a time as the sun dipped behind the lighthouse. Finally, Linda asked the question she most dreaded the answer to.

"And wh-what are you planning to do? I mean, you're almost back to normal, I'm guessing. What, uh, what are your options?"

Light tossed fish bones onto the boardwalk, bringing down a cawing cloud of gulls. "My plan had been to seek out a rebel group of merfolk who are rumored to live in what your people call the Bay of Campeche. Otherwise, I shall have to strike out for the open sea, find a destiny for myself…out there."

"What about—" her voice hitched, and she cleared her throat. "I mean, you said centuries ago some sirens came from the sea and married human men. And we have fairy tales about mermaids becoming human. Can you, I mean, is it possible—"

Light nodded, sighing. "Yes, Linda. There is a very difficult process by which I could become, in essence, human. It is painful and irreversible and highly unlawful."

She winced a bit at his tone. "I was just thinking that, well, I mean, you and me, we seem to have a—"

He turned slowly, looking at her very closely. Gently, he reached out and put his webbed hand on hers. "A connection? Why, yes, Linda. We do. But it would be wrong of me to pursue that."

Her eyes burning, Linda whispered, "Why?"

"Oh, dear friend, for several reasons. My race is long lived. I know I appear to be a boy of near your age, but I have seen more than forty summers. Also, the sea is my home. I cannot imagine living in your world of cars and computers, stores and cellular phones. And though it is difficult to explain, I am a prince, of noble upbringing."

"So I'm beneath you, huh?" She pulled her hand away, the taste of bile in her mouth.

"No, that is not what I meant. In my culture, a noble-born triton and siren bond once for life. Despite the affection I feel toward you, I cannot decide, after only a few weeks of knowing a girl, to undergo a traumatic transformation and dedicate the remainder of my life to her."

Linda drew her legs up to her chest, clutching them tight with her arms. His tone was calm, caring, but his words were brutal in their honesty. She was used to the white lies humans told each other, the way they played pretend. She should have known he would be different. Almost alien.

Still.

"Okay," she breathed into the crook of her arm. "You're too old for me. You don't know me well enough. You don't want to be human. Is there—is there some way I can become like you? Spend more time with you ... out there?"

"Ah, sweet Linda. I am so sorry to have come into your life and caused you this pain. No, Linda. You have no siren blood. I know of no magic that could transform you. And even did I possess such knowledge, I would be reluctant to reveal it. You do not know what awaits in those depths."

Her head and heart ached horribly. She felt that any moment she might explode. It was worse than Robert. She was exposing herself in ways she never had, and Light's refusal was humiliating.

"You don't understand," she gasped. "I—I love you."

Then she was sobbing, and his hands pulled her into the water with him. He embraced her as she wept, stroking her hair like a parent.

"You have so much love to give," he muttered, "and there are others with great need of it. Your father. Your mother. Your friends. The boys you will undoubtedly meet, whose lives will be the better for having experienced your sweet attentions. You have a part to play in life. It is a beautiful role. Do not cower from it."

He released her, pensive and distant. She climbed the netting onto the boardwalk. "Goodnight," she muttered in shame and anger. As she slid the door shut behind her, she thought she heard a sob.

Linda was awakened at 3 am by a phone call from her father. He sounded afraid.

"M'ija, I need your help. Gotta pay 500 bucks to bail me out."

"Bail you out? Dad, are you in jail?"

"Yeah, goddamn cops busted the place where I was—well, you know."

"Uh-huh. Gambling. I get it. Where do you expect me to get five hundred dollars at three in the morning, Dad?"

"Come on, don't you have a little something squirreled away? Un guardadito?"

"You're shitting me. How am I supposed to put money aside when you steal my tips, huh? Gah!"

"Honey, come on, please. Help me out."

She sat there in bed for a few moments, rubbing her eyes.

"Linda?"

"Alright, alright. I've got an idea. Just go lie down in your cell or whatever."

So much for that mayoral bid, Dad. Damn.

After brushing her teeth and changing, Linda called her Grandma Chenta. It took a little while, but she finally explained all the stupid things her father was doing, from cooking the books to gambling.

Her grandmother was angry, but also concerned. "He's my son, and I'll get him straightened out. But I'm going to need your help, Lindita. Can I count on you? It won't be easy, but if we love him, we owe it to him."

"Of course, abuela. Whatever you need."

"Bueno, I'll be by to pick you up in a bit. Then we'll go bail the idiot out."

After ten minutes of waiting, Linda couldn't take it anymore. She strode outside, ready to give Light a piece of her mind.

Selfish, stuck-up fishman, she steamed silently. *Want to know the fury of a woman scorned?*

But the net was empty. The waxing moon, just a week from being full, streamed melancholy silver down, its brilliance swallowed up by the inky green of the Laguna Madre.

"Light?" she called. The only reply was the plashing of waves. Her eyes brimming with tears, she glanced about and saw her scaling knife lying on the pier. She knelt and discovered a message in Spanish carved into the weathered wood.

Tu padre te necesita, y el mío a mí.

Your father needs you, and mine needs me.

Linda remained there, unmoving, until her cell phone started buzzing. When she didn't answer, a text message dinged through. Her grandmother was waiting for her out in front.

But Linda, not moving from her crouch, looked back at the wavering image of the moon on the water, a celestial body that was both foreign and essential to the waves of the sea.

She spoke her thoughts aloud, in case the triton was lingering.

"I'm so tired of people telling me what to do with my life. Men, especially, whether from the land or the ocean. I *know* what I need. What I want. So if you're out there still, listen close, Light. I'm going to help my grandmother. Together, we will somehow rescue my dad from himself."

Linda stood and tossed the knife into the boat.

"And then, you arrogant fucking fishman, I'm going to search high and low for a way. A spell or a potion, a deal with some deity—whatever it takes to transform myself into a siren.

"Not to find you, O Prince of Glowing Grottoes. But because I deserve happiness as much as anyone. And something tells me that mine is waiting for me out there, in the depths of that endless blue."

There was no response, just the purring churn of the Laguna Madre and the sloshing of water against the pier.

Her phone dinged again. Linda shrugged and scoffed.

But as she walked away, the teen could have sworn she heard a stifled sob amid the soft soughing of the waves.

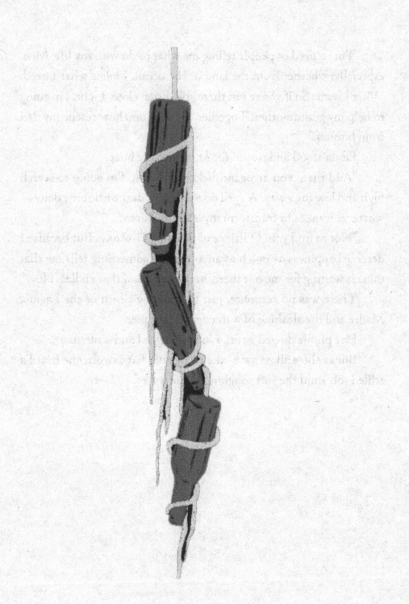

TO BRAVE
THE MOUNTAINS

THE NIGHT THEY TOOK SARAN'S LITTLE BROTHER FROM the ranch was like many other nights on the High Plains: the thin, cold wind keened wildly over the meager yellow grass, herding dark storm clouds in a furious stampede westward across the sky to join the thick mist that shrouded the mountains of Chanor.

Only a few fat drops of moisture spattered the stony soil of what Plainsmen called the Zuduls, the badlands, their promised country. In the thirty-five years since they had first settled on this vast altiplano, rain had never fallen. The clouds just streamed tantalizingly overhead, and the ceaseless wind moaned as if mocking the Plainsmen's travails.

Saran had just been lulled to sleep by the banshee crying of that wind when a pounding at the door jerked her awake. Only tragedy could bring someone to our family's parcel at this late hour, she reflected. And her heart ached with a sudden prescience. For there was a registered skinwalker in her family, one whose ability had just manifested as he reached his twelfth year.

Leaping to her feet, Saran crossed to her brother Mara's bed. She took up his herding crook and stood ready to defend him. The muffled sounds of their mother's distress and their father's anger were soon drowned by the stomping of feet, and the leather curtain across the bedroom entrance was jerked aside unceremoniously by a Chanoripa warrior. He clutched a battle-axe, and the solar corona that swept across his brass helmet marked him as one of the Malyu-kiqu's own honor guard. Two other, lower-ranking men entered with lanterns illuminating their heavily quilted robes, woven from the hair of the very animals Saran's people were permitted to raise.

"Stand aside, girl," the ranking warrior instructed with surprising softness in Runaqu Chima, Chanor's lingua franca. "We've been sent for the boy, and it's useless to defy us."

"You're not taking him," she said. "I won't let you." Her mouth was dry with fear, but she managed to add, "Your rulers won't feast on his soul." She gripped the staff more tightly. She was only fourteen, but she was a Plainsman, and her people had been hardened by five centuries of wandering, enslavement, and oppression.

"Hashams Nurbujun Saran!" Her father's voice rumbled with indignation and hints of remorse. As his bearded face appeared over the warrior's shoulder, Mara yawned groggily from the bed behind Saran. She felt him stiffen suddenly as he took in the tableau.

"Father!" Saran begged in her native tongue. "Let them take me instead!"

His eyes red and his voice hoarse, her father shook his head. "No, Saran. You're not this family's nawa. And we agreed. All the clans agreed."

Mara drew himself from the bed and touched his sister's shoulder. "It's alright, Saran." In his dark grey eyes she saw a wisdom and resignation that shamed her. "For our family, for the clan, for all Plainsmen—I accept my destiny. The God of the Crook is waiting just beyond the horizon for me. It's a blessing to join the Ancient Ones so early."

Saran was strangely disturbed by his words. *Perhaps this is not wisdom. He repeats the sayings of our people, the phrases we intone when tragedy hits us once again. But does he truly understand that he goes to his death? Have we simply trained him to resign himself?*

But she lowered the staff and moved aside. And the warriors gestured to her brother. He took up his jacket, slipped into his boots, pulled a cap down around his ears, and allowed himself to be guided. She followed them into the room of fellowship, and then out the door into the merciless cold. Her mother and father were right behind her. A line of children, boys and girls from all nine clans, stood waiting in the darkness. Mara walked to them and took his place beside Bishirs Zubujun Balal, a girl Saran remembered from last year's Shearing Day celebration. Mara nodded at Balal and then regarded his family with a faint smile.

"One eye on the herd," he called.

His father's voice cracked as he finished the refrain, "The other on the stars."

Compelled by the wind, the line of children moved off into the darkness, toward the looming mountains of Chanor. Saran's heart ached, but she did not weep. She was a Plainsman. Tears were superfluous.

Some little time later, the remaining family sat around a stone table, quietly sipping butter tea. Saran stared at her parents in silence, seething. Her mother's eyes seemed empty. Her father, normally so imposing and robust, seemed sapped of all life.

"This is ridiculous. How could your forefathers agree to this insane practice?" Saran finally demanded.

"Oh, Saran," her father whispered hoarsely. "You know perfectly well. When our people arrived here, five hundred years had passed since we'd left Bodols in hopes of finding a land less ravaged by drought and plagues. We'd spent more than a century as the slaves of the Moundbuilders, only escaping when their arrogant aping of the gods brought a flood that nearly destroyed us as well. Then there were the dark years, the endless trek through Nemeyan, harried and hunted by the Horsemen. Crossing the Great River and mounting this plateau: it was a miracle. Just as the God of the Crook promised. A cold, hard land, but one that we could call our own. Neither Chanor nor Saak really wanted it. The two empires were content, with their final pact of peace, to let us live here."

"At a price," Saran muttered.

"There is always a price," her mother responded. "And it seemed a good one. Skinwalking wasn't something we sought. It was a burden placed on us by the God of the Crook. Families celebrate when a generation goes by without a nawa being born."

"Ah, so sacrificing them so the undead rulers of a tyrannical nation can continue their oppression was better than dealing with them? Than teaching them how to control their transformations, how to keep their inner beast from hurting others?"

"Of course not," her father interjected. "But we had come to the end of our journey. Southward? Southward lie the Wastelands, and we could never hope to cross them. We could not turn back. So, our fathers made the hard choice. My oldest brother was one of the first to be sent to the mountains. Don't think to lecture me, girl, about loss and injustice. I've seen more than you can imagine. We send our nawa children to Chanor, and they let us ranch here, buying up what wool, leather and meat we don't ship over the falls to Saak. It is a truce we can live with."

"Until the God of the Crook guides us to other pastures," intoned her mother.

"Or takes into his flock the rest of the world," her father whispered, completing the verse.

Or bares claws and fangs to rend the world to shreds, Saran bitterly thought as she bid her parents good night.

She lay awake in bed, her mind awhirl with plans. *It will take them close to ten days to reach the city of Chanor, perhaps longer. I have time. But time for what?* She was not, as her father had pointedly remarked, a nawa. She still remembered her brother's first transformation: the rent clothing, the strange fatty sludge, his jaguar hide glistening in the moonlight as their father had looped a guidestick round the beast's neck. She had been horrified, deeply afraid. And relieved. She hadn't been cursed.

Now, she would give anything to have that power.

She kept turning the problem over and over in her mind. If only. Perhaps another family in her clan whose nawa had not yet been taken? But no, she couldn't burden anyone else with saving her brother. It was a task that fell to her.

With a shudder, she discovered a way. She was not a nawa. But she knew of those who could make her become one. Insane. *It's insane.* But the moment she considered the possibility, she knew she had to try.

When her father's deep snoring added its rhythm to the wind's moan, Saran slipped out of bed and into the accounts room. Leather scrolls, knotted strings and concertinaed wooden books were arranged across a table and along the wall. From a pigeonhole she extracted a relatively new scroll and spread it open.

A map. Of the Wastelands.

The sun rose red over broken hills as Saran descended the High Plains on her shabat, following the wending path of the meager, murky Slipsoul River. She napped beside a stunted juniper, but her urgency was too great for any real rest. Despite her mount's complaints, she continued south.

By noon of her second day of travel she reached the desert's edge; the river widened and slowed until it became a pestilent marsh, then stinking black mud, and finally cracked and sterile clay. Now the white sands of the Wastelands spread forbiddingly before her.

Pulling firmly on the long fur of the shabat's hump, Saran dismounted and rested in the miserly shade of a dune while she studied the map and broke her fast with unleavened bread. I'll reach it tomorrow. That leaves seven days. She thought briefly about possible pursuers, but once again she dismissed the possibility. Her father would see she had stolen the map, but he could hardly imagine that she had come south. Everyone would assume she had traveled toward Chanor.

She slept at the foot of the dune, rising at twilight to continue her journey. As dawn eased dark softly from the sky, the horizon seemed to gape, jagged teeth silhouetted against the pink.

The City.

She approached on foot, guiding her mount by its lead. The constructions loomed, dwarfing even in their ruinous state anything mankind had ever built. The ziggurats of Saak, the mountain strongholds of Chanor; neither came close to the overwhelming size and decaying majesty of these shattered monstrosities. Saran forced her eyes down off the bent towers and blasted spires, onto the broad, pitted boulevard. Zigzagging her way around impassable drifts of sand and unrecognizable mounds of time-rotted metal, she kept her senses sharp. The stories say that they remain. I must find one.

For hours she wandered the City's labyrinthine roads, stopping to eat a little and rest for a time before resuming her quest. As afternoon lengthened vast shadows into virtual twilight, she finally saw movement. There. In the entrance to that smaller building. A flash of color. The click of claws on granite.

She flipped the reins around a rusted pole and slipped into the growing gloom. Through doors that had been wrenched free of their moorings she stepped into a vast hall. From the end came a glow, as if of candlelight. As quietly as possible, Saran made her way along the wall until she came to an illuminated room. Peering in, she noted the machinery, the books, the vials and accouterments of an alchemist. And there were other objects beyond her ken, indicating that she had, indeed, found one of them.

A voice hissed harsh clacking syllables, then more clearly pronounced words in Kit'än umaak, the language of Saak. She did not understand.

"Come in, if you must," a raw voice offered in Runaqu Chima. "A human girl in the City. That is a tale that bears hearing."

Saran stepped fully into the doorway just as a figure emerged from an unlit corner of the room. She bit her tongue so as not to gasp.

A large, feathered lizard stood before her, a gauzy robe draped over its rainbow quills. Unfathomable wisdom radiated from its black eyes, and taloned fingers gestured at her with grace and serenity.

"Enter, girl. Urgency is written on you, legible even to an old kurina' who seldom sees a human face, beyond those villains who brave the desert to escape their crimes. It is a home to criminals, this wasteland."

Saran, overcoming her initial awe, approached the kurina'. "So it's true. The people of Saak worship you as Ququmetsh, but you are many."

The creature's tongue flicked at the air. Saran noticed that it did not blink. "And we are not gods. We once believed ourselves close to apotheosis, but we were fools."

"I have heard of your great powers, and I come to make a request." Saran felt foolish for blurting it out like this, but there were now only six days left before her brother's soul would be devoured by the undead rulers of Chanor.

"Request? What is it that you think I can bequeath you? Did you not look about you as you wandered the City? There is no power here. If you only understood how many times the kaurina'a have risen from the ashes of their failure, rebuilt their cities, reached out toward the unknowable depths only to destroy it all, again and again. Is this power? Perhaps. But it is not a thing your people ought come in search of."

"I don't understand what you mean, but I definitely need your help. My brother is a skinwalker, and he's been taken by the honor guard of the Malyukiqu."

The kurnina' gave an aspirated hiss that surely indicated a strong emotion. "The living dead rulers of Chanor will feast on his soul; is that it?"

"Not if I can stop them, they won't."

The alchemist cocked its head like a bird, rapid and inquisitive. "How?"

Saran steeled herself. "I want you to make me a skinwalker, too."

"Why? So that you may attack these guards, rend them to pieces, rescue your kinsman? Is that your plan?"

"No." She took a step toward the feathered lizard. "No, I plan to offer myself in his place."

There was silence then. The large, liquid eyes of the alchemist seemed to bore deeply into Saran's heart, staring frankly at what it discovered, dispassionate and calculating. Then it quickly crossed the rest of the space between them and curled its claws around her forearms.

"What is your name, child?"

"Saran. Hashams Nurbujun Saran."

"One of the Plainsmen. Yes, the animal force is prominent in your souls. Hence the high incidence of skinwalkers among your kind." It flicked its tongue toward her. "Indeed, I believe it can be done."

Saran's eyes suddenly filled with unwanted moisture. "You'll help?"

"I will, child. There is goodness in you alloyed with unexpected mettle. This is less common than you know."

"Thank you. What do I call you? What's your name?"

The feathered lizard leaned in closer, its leathery snout nearly touching Saran's nose. "The kaurina'a have abandoned names. Our arrogance abrogated any right to names long ago. But I am referred to as Tso Nilsi'a: She Who Hopes."

Saran nodded curtly. It was a good title that augured well, even if Tso Nilsi'a refused to see it as her name. The human girl's chest loosened finally, after days of anxiety. *I can do this. I can save his life.*

Strange machines hummed around Saran. Tso Nilsi'a sang haunting, eerie melodies as she obscurely manipulated dials and levers, poured acrid chemicals into hissing vials, sketched ancient runes in bowls full of colored sand. As she'd been warned, Saran's entire body began to feel overly warm. Her skin itched unbearably, every inch of it crawling. Her breath came faster and faster as the hum became a whine and the chanting a series of shouts. Finally, at the center of Saran's being, some hungry part of her pushed, and she fell to the tiled floor, clear of the machines. Clawing at her own flesh, she struggled to free herself, shed this wretched disguise that kept her from tasting the wind as she ran beneath the stars. *Claw it! Claw it away!* And her claws tore loose, and she peeled back the human form with shuddering, excited paws until she stood on all fours, panting hungrily in the darkling light of the saurian's home.

"Do not forget!" Tso Nilsi'a yelled above the raucous noise of the machines. "Your brother's scent: follow it! You are ravenously hungry: eat, soon, and in great quantities. Hold on to this form. And remember: each form contains its opposite, interlocking, complementary, both yearning to be released. But you yourself, you are a whole. You decide which shape to wear. Now go!"

Saran exploded into the night air, her senses drowning in the sharp smells and moonlit contours. Her tawny paws pounded the sand-crusted streets as she rushed northward. She caught the odor of a beast, the shabat, the girl's mount, not the jaguar's. Saran the jaguar had no need of this of beast other than for sustenance.

It was a dumb animal, felled easily, and Saran sated the deep hunger her transformation had caused before tearing off across the silvered dunes toward the hills that led up the edge of the plateau into the mountains of Chanor.

Exhilarated past her human endurance, the jaguar ran for nearly eighteen hours every day, stopping as she came across likely prey in order to feast and sleep and dream the violent dreams of her kind. By the third day she had reached the highland forests of the empire's southern borders, and she caught her brother's scent in a crosswind blowing from a nearby body of water. Dropping to a more cautious gait, Saran made her way along the tree line until she came across a human camp at the edge of what had to be Lake Tiwakara, on the other shore of which would be the priests who would travel the rest of the way with the honor guard and captives, preparing them for their doom.

It was nearing nightfall on the seventh day since Mara had been taken from their home. When she finally saw him, sitting beside Balal, warming himself near the fire, her human form began to push from within. But the jaguar held it back. The guards needed to see the transformation to be convinced.

A light snow had begun to fall when Saran padded into their midst. The Chanoripa warrior who had burst into her home saw her first. He leaped to his feet, drawing his battle-axe and dropping into a crouch. The other guards reacted nearly as fast, drawing weapons and protecting the children.

Saran leaned back on her haunches and let the human form surge forward. Frantically sloughing off the black-spotted pelt, the girl stood naked and steaming in the cold mountain air.

"You," the chief warrior muttered, standing.

"Saran!" Mara rushed to her, pulling his cloak around her. "But you're not a nawa."

"I—I wasn't. Before." She found speaking difficult after so many days as a beast.

Two of the guards pulled them apart. Their leader slid his axe back into its loop and approached Saran.

"I won't ask how your people managed to keep your nature from us. But, having successfully deceived the Malyukiqu and their honor guard, why would you risk our wrath by revealing yourself in this way?"

Saran had not anticipated this interpretation of the facts. Panicked, she rushed to explain. "No, my people haven't lied to you. I wasn't a skinwalker before. I was made one."

Several of the guards made disgusted, dismissive sounds.

"Don't insult me, wench. If skinwalkers could be made, the Empire would have no need of your inferior race. You'd all be dead. Or in prison, waiting to be transformed and your souls imbibed by the Mighty."

"I swear to you. I went into the Wastelands, and a kurina' used her alchemy to make me a nawa."

The guards looked at each other with incredulous faces. Some of them laughed outright. The chief warrior spat his displeasure at the shallow snow.

"What rubbish. But let's pretend for a moment, wench, that you've entered some fairytale world and been made a skinwalker: What is it you want? We are marching thirteen of your kind to the greatest honor mongrels like you can hope for. Is that it? You wish to sacrifice yourself for the glory of Chanor?"

"I want to exchange my life for Mara's. Let him go. I will stay in his place."

"No!" Mara pulled against the guards who held him. "Are you crazy? Go back to the ranch, Saran!"

"Shut up, boy." The Chanoripa warrior shook his head as if unable to believe the situation. He turned to Saran. "Listen closely. I won't be repeating this.

"No. I am not releasing your brother. What's more, you're not going anywhere, either. Something is fishy here, and you're going to answer to the Malyukiqu. Once they're done interrogating you, you'll wish they'd just swallowed your soul.

"But first, you and I are going to have a little chat." Hi eyes travelled down her wrapped body. "I need to have the details of your—transformation transcribed and ready for your audience with the Malyukiqu."

He leaned in close, so only she could hear him. "So unless you have a contingent of magic kaurina'a hiding in the woods there, you are screwed in more ways than one."

The guards grunted their approval. Mara struggled to free himself. The other nawa children stood, aghast, some of them crying.

Saran was less afraid than deeply shamed and angry. I'm so sorry, Tso Nilsi'a. I didn't want this power for this. I would have given my life for him. I swear I would have.

The alchemist's words echoed in her memory: each form contains its opposite, interlocking, complementary, both yearning to be released. But you yourself, you are a whole. You decide which shape to wear.

Saran nodded to herself. I choose the jaguar. The girl can do nothing more.

"Okay," she said aloud. "You'll get your way. I won't put up a struggle. Just, please, can I talk to my brother? In our tongue?"

The chief warrior considered a moment. "Quickly. Then into my tent."

Saran dropped her eyes for a second, and then spoke softly in the coded ranch argot her people had used to befuddle enemies who knew their language, like the fierce Neme of the North. "Listen, all of you. You can shift at will. Our parents never tell us this. They are too afraid. But your animal self is waiting, hungry, wanting to pounce. Don't let them kill you. We don't have to be weak. We have power than none of them has. Why do you think their rulers eat our souls? We are strong. Now, close your eyes and release what longs for freedom!"

She hissed the last command and turned toward the tent. The sun had nearly plunged entirely into the distant sea, and its reddened, feeble light caused the opening to loom darkly. Come on, she pleaded inwardly as she began walking. The warrior was right behind her. He snatched her brother's cloak away. His hand touched her bare flesh as she entered the black.

Screams shot through the twilight. Saran felt her captor tense and turn to leave.

The jaguar shoved its way out, bursting from the girl and sinking its jaws into the guard's throat. When the man's corpse hit the ground, the jaguar skittered out into the snow. Three of the children lay dead in their human forms. Ten cats of varying sizes and color were clawing and biting and batting the dying guards, whose screams faded with the last light of the sun.

One by one Saran's pride abandoned their prey and came to stand before her. Looking at them, she could not fathom, neither with her human or animal mind, why anyone so beautiful and so powerful would ever cower in fear on sterile ranches, awaiting death.

We were meant to run free, she thought. To wander the world and take what we need, fearing nothing, obeying no one.

Wordlessly she looked toward the south and then turned her glimmering eyes back to the smaller jaguar, her littermate. Mara whisked his spotted tail, twitched his ears. The other nawa followed suit.

They all agreed. With a jubilant growl, Saran exploded into motion, thundering back into the woods, running southward.

Her pride followed.

SHATTERED INTAGLIO

"I F YOU DON'T HURRY, MARYU, YOU WILL NOT GET TO SEE THE general speak. Your father will expect you to be there."

Maryu Maarcu Aivandor reluctantly walked away from the street performers to follow his tutor, glancing back several times to see if he could catch the end of their farce. The people around the cart exploded with laughter, and Maryu cursed silently, irritated at Sumar for not giving him just a few more minutes to enjoy the performance. He didn't need to be reminded of his responsibilities. Hadn't he been studying the family affairs closely, learning the role that he would eventually take on? He was the eldest son, and he did what was expected of him. So what was so wrong with wanting to be a child from time to time? To laugh long and hearty, especially during as festive a day as this?

The streets were thick with crowds; several times Maryu lost sight of Sumar, but he didn't worry. They were both heading toward the Temple of Dyupadar, and that colossal structure dominated the architecture of the city. Street vendors, recognizing his station and family, offered him food and goods. Maryu just bowed his head politely and refused, hurrying toward the special meeting of the Cosatragana, the highest legislative body in the Republic of Baratu.

Soon he found himself mounting the marble steps, thrusting hurriedly through the throng to find a position on the patio near enough to the open doors—massive, bronze, ancient—to afford him a decent view of the rostrum. As he squeezed into a choice spot beside an ornately carved column, the great Hero of the Republic was welcomed to the temple by the slow, ritual clapping of the legislators.

Joining the general on the rostrum was his brother, Socar Gaumuran Augastya, one of the two mantuni elected last year to preside jointly over the executive functions of the Republic. Socar Gaumuran raised his hand to request silence, and even the hushed conversations on the temple patio were stilled.

"Baratu," the mantu began, "both republic and capital, have today received General Ramul Gaumuran Augastya with great pomp and circumstance, hailing in a majestic parade his victorious military campaign in the northernmost reaches of the continent. The quirita has been placed upon his head, and that feathered ceremonial crown declares him ritual king for a day. So now, as is his right, the Hero of the Republic will address this august body."

Socar Gaumuran inclined his head toward his younger brother. "General."

Ramul Gaumuran stepped forward as his brother left the rostrum. His burnished mail glittered in the afternoon sun that streamed in through the doors; his purple cape swirled about him like a living thing with each precise movement he made. The quirita encircled his dark brow like a promise of national fidelity. His every word, Maryu knew, would have the weight of a god's.

"Fathers, your numerous assembly has always seemed to me the most agreeable body that any man can address, and this hallowed temple has always struck me as the most distinguished place for delivering an oration. I have been prevented from trying this road to glory—open to every son of Baratu—not indeed by my own will, but by the martial life which I adopted as a teen. Before today I would not have dared, on account of my limited achievements, to intrude upon the authority of this place with my own vision for the Republic's future. I felt strongly that no arguments ought to be brought to this place except they be the fruit of great ability and accomplishment. As a result, I have thought it fit to devote all my time to the vanquishing of Baratu's enemies.

"Your most humbling display of recognition today suggests that I have nearly reached that goal."

There was thunderous applause from the patio, and the legislators shook their purple stoles to indicate their approval.

"I say nearly," the general continued as the sound faded, "because the barbarians of the north are not our greatest foe. For millennia another people have harried Baratu, beached ships on our shores, pillaged our towns, burned our temples, raped and razed as they pleased. Six centuries ago we pacted peace with that nation, but as with a disease that goes into remission, lulling the infirm into believing themselves cured until the plague returns, redoubled in virulence, in some other part of their flesh—so the island kingdom has returned to its imperialistic customs, forging alliances with the northern barbarians, providing weapons and armor and logistical support, helping those savages to raid the border regions of our Republic. The seven-year campaign that you entrusted me to wage has extirpated the vermin from our lands. We have installed territorial governors in the conquered chiefdoms.

"But the true root of this blight remains. Lenki. Sea-locked kingdom of filthy idolaters. Safe-haven for pirates and rebels. Moral cesspool in which every abomination is indulged and celebrated. As long as Lenki stands, Baratu is in danger of falling.

"So, Fathers, what I propose is quite simple. Rather than disband the army you put under my command, dispersing the regiments and rerouting the funding, gather together every ship in our fleet sturdy enough to serve as a troop transport, load my soldiers and our materiel, and let us ply the wine-green waves of the sea till we land upon Lenki's beaches and sweep across the island like a monsoon!"

The patio erupted in a chaos of applause, cheers, chants and stomping of feet. Many legislators stood, fanning their chasubles in a sign of support. Some, however, including Maryu's father, remained seated, soberly awaiting their turn to speak. The boy had been privy to many of his father's conversations with important citizens, and he understood that his family was firmly opposed to military action against Lenki, partially because of business interests on the island, but also because the Augastya clan's motives were not nearly so noble as the general was portraying them. And finally, as the Aivandor motto had declared for two thousand years, the sword must be our last resort.

A man near Maryu leaned toward a companion and barked, "It's the general's goras, it is. I hear tell he magicks his enemies, compels them to surrender or make mistakes. That's why he's been so successful, in war and in politics. He's a gorator."

Even at eleven years of age, Maryu knew this was nonsense. The general may indeed have been an adept mage, but he needed no incantations to control the legislators today. The force of his deeds and the reputation of his family were sufficient to sway them as he wished.

General Ramul Gaumuran Augastya wanted Baratu to invade the vast island nation of Lenki. And so it would.

But it was clear that Maryu's father would not sit idly by while his fellow legislators, drunk on the successes in the north, shattered the six-hundred-year peace that had existed between the two mighty nations. So after the more senior legislators had praised the general and his audacious plan for attacking Lenki, Marcu Laugyu Aivandor stood and opposed the invasion. He cited the treaties, the law, the opinions of past leaders; he painted gruesome scenarios of the cost to citizens both in lives and in money; and finally he quoted from the *Verbuni Siduanes*, the sacred Words of the Prophet:

"Il Sidu himself told us, brothers, 'Defend your loved ones and yourself when evil crosses the threshold of your home; otherwise, leave your enemies in the hands of the First Father.' This is a precept of the Way. The general has defended us, and we bend our knee in thanks. But war with Lenki violates all we hold dear, and it will turn the First Father's eyes from us, leaving us open to destruction. We must continue to seek a diplomatic solution to this conflict. Lenki needs our crops and our timber; it craves our silk and our steel. As I have urged in the past, let us restrict trade or completely impose an embargo. Bloodshed is unnecessary."

Maryu's chest began to ache as he listened to his father speak. Marcu Laugyu Aivandor was legislator for the Aivandor clan, his seat in the Cosatragana assured for life by virtue of his being the pre-eminent male in one of the original fifty families.

But that seat might soon be vacant, for his present speech was endangering his life.

Maryu noticed with a shiver that Ramul looked upon his father with eyes full of spite as the man ceded the floor to the next legislator, a wealthy citizen from the Calinga region who reacted vehemently against Marcu Laugyu's message, quoting passages from the *Verbuni* that prophesied the destruction of Lenki at the hands of a mighty bull. Other legislators took up the cry to fulfill the Prophet's vision, while only a handful of legislators opposed their bellicose brethren.

At one point, as the general's face grew more and more contented, he looked through the open door at the crowd in the patio and on the steps. His eyes fell upon Maryu, and though there was no reason that leader of men should recognize the boy, Maryu knew he did. Immediately his hands went to his chest, clasping the medallion, his fingers tracing the warding runes embossed upon the silver triangle. Ramul's goras probed him, tentative at first, and then insistent. Maryu muttered an apasinte to strengthen the runes, and he felt the general's touch withdraw. The warrior nodded his head and smiled more broadly.

Sumar the tutor tugged at his robes at that moment, as if he'd noticed the exchange of power between the boy and the man. "Come, young master. Time we returned to your home and shared the day's experiences with your brother."

Maryu allowed his tutor, a slave from some northern nation who had been with his family for decades, to guide him home through the still ebullient streets of Baratu. Once free from the long shadow of the temple's tower, they wound their way ever upward, past the vast marketplace and the Hill of Victory, alongside the massive divipas in which hundreds of working-class families lived in cramped squalor.

At the stables near the Sunatra bathhouse a carriage waited, ready to take Maryu and his tutor through the High Gate and along the wending road to the plateau. As the packed earth gradually leveled out, Maryu turned and looked down upon the capital city, sprawled like a drowsy predator across the hills to the south of the otherwise inaccessible high plains of the Adyaru region. His incipient vertigo was stilled by a sense of awe.

Near the edge of the plateau, crisscrossed by rainbows refracted by late afternoon sunlight slanting through the spray from the falls, the Aivandor estate spread greenly, open to wind and sky. Maryu regarded the ancient, bleached stone of the family villa and awe gave way to sudden confident pride. For two thousand years his family had served Baratu, first its kings and then its citizens. There was nothing to fear from a scheming general. His father was safe.

As soon as he crossed under the complex arches of the entryway, his younger brother Laxman greeted him with rapid-fire questions.

"Tell me about the parade! Was it really big? What did the general's armor look like? Did they crown him? Did you see any jesters? What about the street plays? Come on, Maryu, tell me what you saw!"

"Slow down, Lax. I've been walking and riding for two hours. Give me a moment, will you?" He dropped onto a chair and sighed. "The parade was fantastic. Everyone in the city was there, and the general rode an elephant at the head of his troops. Streamers were everywhere, and the music was loud. He had on his mail and a purple cape with gold fringes. And yes, the mantuni presented him with the feathered crown.

"As for the streets, they were crowded, and there were jesters and jugglers and street actors. People just gave me food when they saw the family insignia brocaded on my robe."

Laxman pouted for a moment. "It's not fair I couldn't go. You're only a year older than me."

"Sixteen months," Maryu corrected.

"Like it matters. I had to stay here and listen to mother ordering the Narsimyuni about with that tone she uses when she's nervous for Father."

Maryu closed his eyes for a moment till a vision of Ramul's smile made him open them with a start. "She's got good reason to, Lax. The general wants to invade Lenki. That's what he announced at the end of his speech to the Cosatragana. But Father publicly opposed him, and I could see the general was furious."

"And…and Ramul tried to get at me with his goras."

Laxman gaped in astonishment. "Why would he want to magic you?"

"I don't know. Maybe… maybe he wants to get at Father. He might've been trying to push a niyurinte at me, force me to do something bad to Father. Who knows? But my wardings held, and he seemed impressed."

"Mother always said you had God's touch stronger than the rest of the family. Throwback to our great-grandfather Uvid, she says, remember?"

Before he could respond, Numat, the youngest narsimyu slave at the villa, brought a tray of fruit and cheese in, setting it on a table near the two brothers.

"Goras is strong in young master," he muttered in his hoarse simian voice. "Numat feels it even with the collar blocking his heart's eye."

Maryu examined Numat closely. The ape-like creature had gold fur fretted with orange, like many of his race, and the bare skin of his palms and face was pale, nearly pink. Around his neck was clamped the silver collar which ensorcelled every narsimyu in the Republic, the intricate intaglio of runes carved upon the metal dampening the simians' supernatural abilities.

"Wait. You can sense my goras?"

"Yes. Numat has felt it grow in young master lo these several years. Very special goras, too. Narsimyuni call it *urreke*. Baratuans say *shattering*."

Maryu's breath caught in his throat. Shattering was a rare magic indeed, less common even than the general's compelling.

"Sacred balls!" blasphemed Laxman excitedly. "Mar, if you can shatter, that will be amazing!"

"Wait. Don't get all worked up just yet, Lax. Uh, Numat? How is it you know that my goras is shattering?"

"Because urreke is also Numat's magic. Before traders put a collar on this neck, Numat shattered many bones. Killed one. But the price for narsimyuni is very high. The trader boss decided it was worth a dead colleague. And, indeed, Master Marcu did pay many gold coins for Numat. Very prestigious, it is, to have narsimyuni in damu. Very much the fashion."

Laxman was probably too enthused to notice, but Maryu heard the bitterness and ire undergirding the simian's unusually long speech.

"Enough."

He was the child of a ganán, after all, eldest son of a tatalyu of the Republic, a descendant of Ivandor, one of the original founders. He could hardly permit an animal slave to comport himself thus in his presence.

"Go, Numat. You've spoken out of turn, and with too much familiarity. Go! Hurry up now, before I decide to tell my father how out-of-line you're acting."

But Maryu's father never came home that evening. Foreboding grew in the boys' hearts. Their mother paced and fretted and raised her voice at the slaves. Finally, at the sixteenth hour, stars occluded ominously by northern clouds, a messenger came with the devastating news: Ganán Marcu Laugyu Aivandor had been robbed and killed in an alleyway as he journeyed homeward.

Maryu spent the next five days in an emotional fog. The drummers marched from the Aivandor estate to the Temple of Dyupadar, thudding a mournful tattoo to honor the passing of a well-respected tatalyu. Priests of the Way prepared Marcu Laugyu's body with unguents and mantras against corruption; mantratores and goravantes with varying skills guarded his corpse against black magic and dark forces for the halfweek that it lay in state upon the stone bier at Heaven's Hill. Ramul Gaumuran Augastya was one of the most expressive of the mourners, and when the procession finally carried Marcu Laugyu's lifeless form out of the city, across the Dyuvor River, and onto the Plain of Cremation, the general led the way, the grieving widow clinging to his arm. Maryu's heart began to smolder with rage at this dissembling, at the avuncular way Ramul stroked the hair of Maryu's little sister Tula, at the feigned solemnity with which he watched Lidya Marcai Cautoman take up her temporary place upon the pyre at her dead husband's side while a priest intoned the prayer that released her from her death debt.

Every new expression of false grief was pitch tossed upon the flames of hate in Maryu's soul.

You killed my father, whoreson. His mother descended. You hired some shit-heeled scum to wait in the shadows. The priests touched torches to the wood. You paid off the Cosatragana guards that accompany him home. Flames licked at his father's form. They abandoned him at the agreed-upon time and place. Black smoke roiled toward heaven. And then you reached out through your pawns and killed him.

Everyone knows. But no one will touch you.

Except me, you bastard. Somehow. Just wait.

A week passed before Laxman would speak to anyone. When he came to Maryu, his eyes red and empty, the older boy nodded. "Yes. It was the general."

"What are you going to do about it?"

"I'm going to get revenge."

"How?" There was a little surge of hope, of life, in Laxman's pinched features.

Maryu's voice cracked as he muttered, "I'm going to shatter him."

"But you... you don't know how."

"No, but Numat does. Go get him. Don't let anyone know what you want him for. Be quick."

Laxman, purpose brightening his face and lightening his stride, hurried off in search of the narsimyu. Maryu tried, as he had for days, to access the power that Numat had sensed in him. When he reached within himself, however, his sight was blocked, thrust aside by a wave of rage and sadness and bitterness. Again and again he dove, only to be driven out of his trance by more and more powerful barriers, as if his frustration itself amplified his impotence.

"Young master goes about it all wrong."

Through bleary eyes, Maryu looked at Numat, his sleek animal head proud and serene above his silver collar. "What do you mean?"

"Must empty the self first. Anger can come later, once the shattering begins. Anger makes it stronger, less focused, more destructive. But to spark it, you must be empty."

Maryu despaired at ever draining the rage from his soul. It didn't seem possible. It didn't seem right.

"Can you teach me?"

"Yes. But."

"But what?"

Numat lifted a wrinkled finger to the glittering runes at his neck. "Numat would be free, young master. That is his price. And he has heard the rumorings. Not much time is left before the general crosses the sea to Lenki. You must act soon. You cannot act without Numat's help. And Numat demands freedom. The collar, broken."

It was illegal. So was assassinating a general. If Maryu were caught, he would be banished or worse.

It was an easy choice.

"Agreed."

The weeks passed. Lidya Marcai and her daughter Tula remained in the women's wing, as they would all year in obedience to the Way, mourning the passing of the head of the family. With the assistance of his tutor and his father's secretary, Maryu spent the mornings overseeing the family's affairs—the fields, orchards, ships, shops—

and receiving the favors and petitions of certain members of lower castes for whom Marcu Laugyu had been a patron.

Each afternoon, though, he went into the garden and trained. Numat's harsh, hoarse whisper insinuated itself into his mind, guiding him, calming him, helping him loosen the net that bound up his ability. After days of failure, the narsimyu taught him a mantra of serenity, a series of syllables in the simian tongue that meant nothing to Maryu, but that stilled his mind, nonetheless.

And in the stillness, he found the spark, a warm glow in the darkness. It took Numat another week to help him see the fine threads that connected that spark to the world around him.

Finally came the day, three weeks after his father's murder, when Maryu took hold of his goras and sent a thrumming down the threads that led to a nearby mango tree. A loud crack made him open his eyes with a start: a limb of the tree had split lengthwise.

"Good," Numat murmured in response to Maryu's excitement. "But not enough. General will be pushing back, young master. And General is accompanied at all times by nirodores skilled at suppressing the goras of a would-be assassin. To shatter, you will have to push past mighty barriers. Now focus and try again. You must burst the very core of this tree."

Maryu could not. Afternoons stretched into evenings. The boy hardly slept. He split stones, cracked branches, snuffed the lives of lizards and birds.

The tree remained standing. Fruit lay about it, exploded by his efforts. Roots were exposed from the magical push of his mind. But three days before the army of Baratu was to set sail for Lenki, the tree was still intact.

Laxman stood before his older brother, a question in his eyes. Maryu looked away. Numat shook his head.

"He is not ready, little lord. Numat has tried, but there is not sufficient time."

"What? No! We can't let Ramul get away with this!"

Maryu lifted a hand weakly as if to silence his brother, but he was stopped by the narsimyu's soft growl.

"There is another way."

The sons of Marcu Laugyu Aivandor leaned toward the slave, expectant.

"A trick. You attack him with your goras. The nirodores are distracted trying to repulse the samruyante. And then Numat reaches out and shatters general."

Maryu shook his head, not in refusal, but to clear his thoughts. He regarded the silver collar that matted Numat's pale fur, the strange red blotches in the whites of his eyes.

"How do I know you'll help me even after I release you? What's to keep you here? What's to keep you from shattering anyone who tries to stop you from leaving?"

Numat's breath hissed with barely repressed anger. "Ngerre… narsimyuni, we keep our word. Our word binds us. You know nothing! Your people snare us and bind us and think yourselves strong. Bah! Do you hear Numat? Our word binds us."

"Then give us your word," Laxman said.

"Kupu homari. Word given."

Maryu nodded once; he reached within and then without.

The silver collar clattered to the floor.

The streets were teeming. The city was surging toward the Hill of Victory, from whose summit General Ramul Gaumuran Augastya would lead his army on a three-day march to the port town of Corga. From there they would sail across the Middle Sea to making landing on the shores of Lenki.

The two boys, accompanied by Numat, pushed their way through the crowds to get closer to the general. The narsimyu's collar had been reassembled with hoof glue; a strong tug would pull it apart again. They approached the vanguard of the army, where Ramul sat astride a massive destrier, surrounded by his contingent of nirodores, each mounted on a rune-branded rouncey. Numat quickly crossed to the other side of the stone-cobbled Pontín Masemu, acting as if he were buying a bag of roasted nuts for his master. Maryu positioned himself right at the edge of the highway and turned so that he had the general in his line of sight. Laxman stood a couple of paces behind him.

After a trumpet blast, the army began its slow procession. Seconds later, Ramul's steed was within the range of Maryu's goras. When Maryu shut his eyes to search, the general's spark fairly leapt at him, hungry dark flames that licked at the weft of the world. With a cry of fury, Maryu send his shattering along the skein that joined him tenuously to his father's murderer. Immediately the nirodores drew their mounts about; with ducks of the head, mantras and hand signs they deflected his attack. The recoil was a mailed fist striking his forehead: Maryu collapsed like so much dead weight, barely able to remain focused on the champing horses and the face of his brother, bent close to him, muttering questions that the older boy could not hear.

Straining his eyes at the gaps between horses, Maryu was able to make out the form of Numat: the Narsimyu had discarded his broken collar, and his face was twisted with a rage that would have made Maryu tremble were he not so innervated by his own reflected shattering. As his mind teetered on the verge of darkness, the boy felt a long-pent-up wave of terrifying power ripple across reality.

Screams sounded faintly in his deaf ears, and then he understood the true cost of revenge.

The simian's rage was too great, and years of enslavement had eroded his control. The general's nirodores were indeed shattered, bone and blood blossoming outward in a spherical blast. But the thrumming puissance was unfocused, broadcast wildly, and dozens of bystanders crumpled like discarded marionettes, their limbs unnaturally akimbo.

And before Maryu's eyes, tumbling down in the dusty road, Laxman fell lifeless.

Icy knives wrenched at his innards. Bereft, he surrendered himself to the oblivion of unconsciousness, his eyes dropping shut, blocking out the horror.

Then he was wrenched to his feet, slapped back to awareness. Soldiers had hold of him, were shaking him and shouting. His bones ground painfully together.

Ramul was standing over Numat, their magicks locked in a struggle that made the fabric of the cosmos howl about them.

A grin split the general's face of a sudden, and the narsimyu tottered, blood streaming from his eyes, nose, mouth, pores.

With a groan, he crumpled, dead and broken.

Maryu's hearing was coming back, a ringing roar of sound. The cries of the multitude, mainly, gathered weeping around their fallen friends and family.

"Kill him!" came the screams as the citizens of Baratu gestured wildly at Maryu, overcome with grief and rage. "Kill him!"

Maryu was amazed to see Ramul shake his head and raise his hand, demanding silence.

"The boy was consumed by grief," the general called out above the hushing din. "The one he loved the most was taken from him by the will of God. Ah, vainly does Man strive to find human targets for his anger at the First Father's plans. I hear your righteous rage, compatriots. But soft, now. I was the intended victim, after all. The law lays justice for this attempted murder in my hands. If I choose to forgive, who can gainsay me?"

No one spoke. Sullen eyes sparked in the morning sun.

"Of course, your losses must be compensated. Let the boy stand trial for the unintended deaths, the collateral damage. The holdings of the Aivandor are vast; dismantled, they will help to ease your grief."

For a moment, the general held them all by the power of his will alone. Then a mother rushed screaming from the crowd, swinging a club that smashed into Maryu's head.

The darkness took him at last.

"Wake, boy."

Maryu rose up through layers of black, struggling toward the dazzling white of consciousness. He heard soft, muted sounds all around him: padded steps, rustling fabrics. The smell of herbs and unguents hung thickly.

A healer's hall. He gently moved his limbs. If at some point they'd been broken, the healer's skill had mended them.

"Open your eyes, Maryu Maarcu Aivandor."

The general's voice. Alive.

Slowly, unwillingly, Maryu obeyed. The villain grinned down at him. He still wore his mail and purple cloak, which suggested that only a few hours had passed.

"Good boy. I must admit, you've impressed me. Not many of my enemies have gotten as close as you to ending my life. I suspected you might try, but using your narsimyu… well, that was the mark of a true tactician. Of course, it cost you dearly. Three dozen innocent bystanders. Your own brother."

His voice hoarse, Maryu moaned, "Your fault. Bastard."

There was a predatory glitter in Ramul's eyes. He gave a brittle laugh. "You'll have plenty of time to meditate on blame, boy. It's been arranged. Once the trial is over, you'll be sent to a monastery in the North. To join the Palitas Order in their devotion to the Way."

Maryu rose on his elbows, his distress boiling away as hatred surged from within.

"With your brother dead and you in exile, what remains of the Aivandor estate, after the jury awards the families of the dead, will fall to me. It may be that your widowed mother, once my victory is secure and her bereavement over, will consent to be my bride."

It was too much to bear. Maryu balled his hands into fists, tried to attack with body and soul, but his goras would not respond. It was as if all power had been stripped from him. Ramul pushed him back onto the bed with a sigh.

"It's unfortunate. At the temple, I sensed such potential in you. I could have honed you like a sword, used your keen edge in battle. But you'll never wield magic again, Maryu Maarcu Aivandor. Never."

The boy's hands went to his neck then, groping in spasms, and found runes carved upon a silver collar, dumb yet ineluctable words that silenced the spark of his heart.

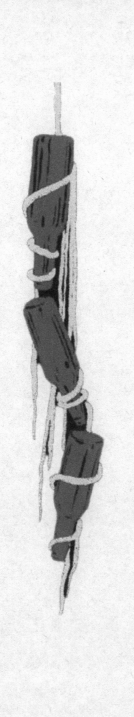

DAVID BOWLES is a Mexican American author and translator from South Texas, where he works as an associate professor at the University of Texas Río Grande Valley. Among his three dozen award-winning books are *The Smoking Mirror*, *The Witch Owl Parliament*, *They Call Me Güero*, *My Two Border Towns*, *Ancient Night*, and *The Prince & the Coyote*. David presently serves as the president of the Texas Institute of Letters.